November in America:

A Story of Thanksgiving

by Nicholas Bernhard

Colorado's Northern Coal Field 1927

Baseline Road (40 degrees North)

LOUISVILLE

Acme Mine

The Marshall Mesa
Coal discovered here 1856

SUPERIOR

Industrial Mine

Southern Coal Fields 200 Miles South

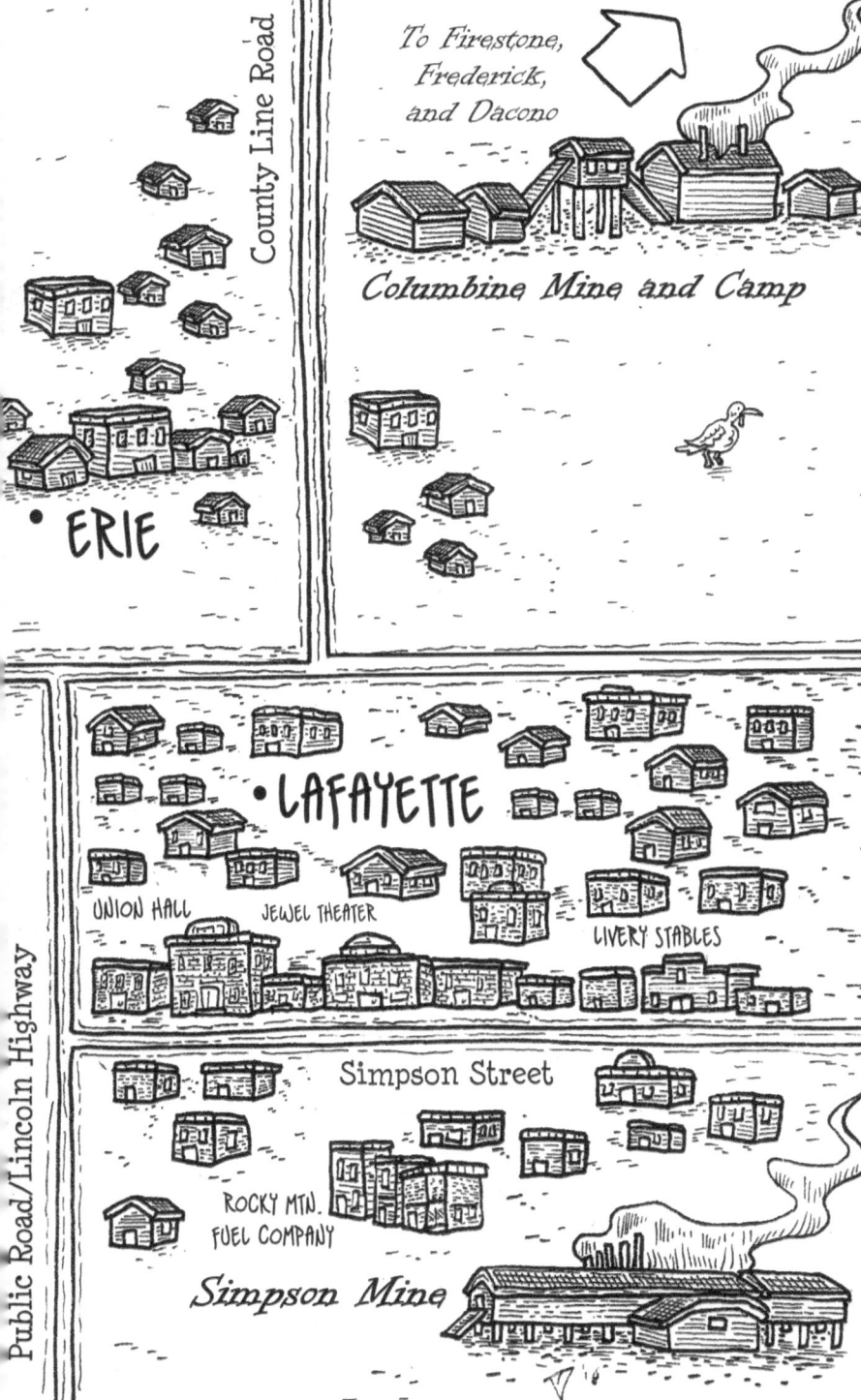

DISCLAIMER

This is a work of fiction. It is inspired by actual events that took place between Labor Day and Thanksgiving of 1927, in the northern and southern coal fields of Colorado. However, it is not intended as an objective or authoritative account of these events.

Even when characters and incidents share the names and circumstances of actual people and historic events, this does not change the fictional nature of the work.

In all other respects, any resemblance to real-life people, places, or events, is entirely coincidental.

Table of Contents

For Mom and Dad

"O beautiful for pilgrim feet,

Whose stern impassion'd stress

A thoroughfare for freedom beat

Across the wilderness!

America! America! God mend thy ev'ry flaw,

Confirm thy soul in self-control

Thy liberty in law!"

   - Katherine Lee Bates, 1904

PROLOGUE

or, The Not-So-Long-Ago

On the front walkway of the Bob Burger Recreation Center, a giant inflatable turkey sways in the November wind. "The 4th Annual Cold Turkey Run," proclaims its girthing midsection, "5K fun-run for childhood vaccinations. Free clinic inside." The morning sun shines a crisp, hard light in the sky. This being November in Colorado, the sun will be generous enough to stick around for a few more hours, before plunging the world into darkness around 5 PM.

Across the parking lot, middle-schoolers on Thanksgiving Break navigate their way through the bowls and rails of the skate park. The baseball diamond lies empty. Toddlers run giddy toward piles of cottonwood leaves.

The Recreation Center sits in the heart of Lafayette, a smallish city north of the Denver metropolis, and east of the Republic of Boulder. To the middle-school skateboarders, Lafayette was a doldrum of pretty parks, farmer's markets, trailer courts, and oatmeal festivals.

Nothing was open after 8 PM, and the popular pastime was driving to the neighboring town of Louisville, to get a poster framed at Hobby Lobby. The main attraction was a massive, market-tested megachurch, based out of an old Wal-Mart, which doubled Lafayette's population every weekend.

On the far end of the Recreation Center's parking lot, and far from the mind of anyone on a skateboard, sits the Lafayette Cemetery. Its marble headstones are visible from the Center's second-story running track, serving as motivation for the regular power-walkers.

Two skateboards roll out of the park, and are kicked up into the arms of Sean and Gerry, friends since the third grade. Sean lives in the Old Town neighborhood, a ten-minute's walk from the skate park. Old Town was a grid of minuscule houses packed like Manhattan subway trains, houses that grew more cracked and creaky with every new rainstorm. Gerry will follow him as far as the bus stop, and hitch a ride to the Blue Heron suburb on the edge of town. In English class, he had endured half a semester of Greek tragedy, and so he relished the thought of fifteen minutes on a bus, where he could read *A Dance With Dragons*. Now *there* was some literature.

Sean speaks up. "I heard Connor is going to Vail with his family for Thanksgiving Break."

And wouldn't it figure, thinks Gerry. "Lucky him. Probably has his own place up there, the 'winter home.'" Gerry knew this was true, in fact, and had asked Connor when he might be able to join him, and play paintball on his 200-acre ranch. "And I get to spend another Thanksgiving break in Lafayette."

"I mean, I'll be here tomorrow," says Sean, "and maybe we can play some ice hockey in Louisville…"

Gerry responds with cricket noises.

"All right, whatever," says Sean, adding with a smirk, "This week, I'm just going to be thankful for all I've been given."

Gerry smiles. "Yee-up. Let's just be thankful for a safe, sterile holiday, devoid of all fun and excitement."

"Thankful for week of watching my grandpa yell at football games," adds Sean, "and another year of rejection from Sofía."

"Another holiday dinner, listening to Mom and Aunt Valerie argue politics," says Gerry, "and the same three movies on TV, because Thanksgiving is the world's most boring holiday, and I live in the world's most boring town."

Sean wasn't sure what made him look over at the cemetery then. Maybe he thought it odd the mist in the cemetery hadn't burned off yet, especially as it was so dry this time of year. Sean realizes Gerry is watching him stare at the cemetery. It was just too dumb.

Sean laughs, and says, "And this is the part where the Ghost of Christmas Past comes out and attacks me, right?"

"But of course!" says Gerry, who yells out to the rows of headstones, "You wanna piece of this, ghost? Come at me, bro!"

The next voice they hear belongs to neither Sean nor Gerry. A voice coming from the tall bushes they had just passed, giving them a heave of terror that curls their insides up until breakfast, started coming up again.

"No ghosts, my friend, only a creature of the night."

Turning to see the diseased man behind them turns their legs to jelly, their throats too dry to scream. His skin was devoid of color, and thick mats of black hair, home to every local species of insect, run down to his ragged, reeking clothes. This pale (no, *uncolored*) man steps out of the bushes, off the curb, and takes a very polite bow.

"Good morning. I am Fodor Glava: coal miner, vampire, and guardian spirit of Lafayette. I came here, all the way from Transylvania, to work deep down in the labyrinth shafts far below us."

Sean looks over at Gerry, and sees the same mix of terror and confusion he was sure covered his own face. Yes, this was really happening.

The vampire continues. "I died of the Spanish Influenza and they threw my body in the communal grave like some plague-ridden livestock! For one hundred years now, I have kept watch over this city, and now, the time has come that I would have words with you."

Gerry, who has survived middle school so far by trying to make people laugh, snaps his fingers. "Wait a minute, you're not like those pretty-boy vampires I've seen in the movies."

The vampire, apparently named Glava, laughs, and it sounds like a diesel engine full of sludge. "Believe me, kid, you do not want me to take my shirt off. No, I am here to take the wool off of your eyes! That peace and quiet you find so painfully boring was won with a lot of sweat, and more than a little blood."

Gerry finds some of his courage restored, and challenges the vampire. "Sweat and blood, huh? You mean cowboys, prospectors, hard winters, *Little House on The Prairie* stuff?"

Sean joins in. "That's old news. This is Colorado, name me one town out here that doesn't have those stories."

Glava shakes his head, coughing up a few more decades of phlegm. "No, no! This is no ordinary land, children. This is *coal country*. The men and women who lived here, in the Not-So-Long-Ago, changed all your lives... forever!"

The vampire Glava arches his back, raising his arms to the sky. "Spirits! I call upon you this cold November morn!"

Thunder cracks in the blue sky. Wind blows the rock-hard cottonwood leaves into a swirling funnel.

"These children have forgotten the faces of their forefathers! People no longer remember the stories of old! I summon the spirits of this cemetery to roll back the years, to speak and live as you did then."

The sky dances, the cars race backward home, and the spirits of the cemetery clutch the feet of their own headstones to pull themselves from the earth. They hurry left and right, and soon a hulking tower of wood is rising above the evergreens. Gerry recognizes the movements of the spirits: he's seen it before in theater class. The undead souls are putting on a performance for them.

"Spirits!" cries Glava, "Tell us of your harshest sorrows, and most joyous delights! Spirit us across time, to a little camp nestled in the hills: the Columbine Mine!"

Sean and Gerry watch the years roll back, and as the spirit's ethereal stage is set, Glava sings the song of his city:

"Through blistering deserts and bone-chilling rain,

They came from all corners to a treeless plain

On steamships and wagons, to where mountains look down,

There were jobs to be had, deep underground.

The road to the schoolhouse was worn and unpaved,

Wives prayed each morning their husbands be saved

With ghost stories whispered by the kerosene lamp,

While miners talked home through the mist, cold and damp,

Battle the sadness with laughter and mirth,

When a day's journey west seemed the ends of the Earth,

Work for a living in the darkness below,

How strange it all seems... but it was not so long ago.

There was so very little on which to depend

Except love from your family, or kindness from friends,

To protest one's lot was a dangerous crime

A coal miner must know his place, and that place is the mine.

In churches and dance halls, the music ran wild,

There were stories and legends in the mind of each child,

Spiting the fear, how the choir would sing,

Here, in the tenement camp, coal is king,

Battle the sadness with laughter and mirth,

When a day's journey west seemed the ends of the Earth,

Work for a living in the darkness below,

How strange it all seems... but it was not so long ago."

OCTOBER, 1927.

Charles Lindbergh is a worldwide hero.

Construction has begun on Mount Rushmore.

Joseph Stalin has seized power in the Soviet Union.

In America, alcohol is illegal, but underground drinking persists.

Women have had the right to vote for seven years.

CHAPTER ONE

The Morning Shift

The steam whistle pierces through the gray light of morning. The whistle carries over the autumn mist, over the rolling hills of the Columbine Mine, and back home to Lafayette. Little Dorothy will be headed to school now, thinks John Eastenes. His wife Bertha knows the Columbine blows its whistle ten minutes before the school bell back in Lafayette, so it helps keep Dorothy on time. The black beams of the mine tipple rise over the work line. Most miners took it as a given it would fall over on them someday, most likely on their last day of work. Eastenes hopes not, he has other plans.

Eastenes has stood in the work line for the past three days, and not once has his number been called. Three days, with his dented lunch bucket rattling against his overalls in one hand, a pickaxe in the other, the old wood worn shiny from years of his iron grip. He needs this. Last night, he prayed that his number be called, with a follow-up prayer on the six-mile walk to the Columbine. What worries Eastenes, though, is that even if the Lord Above is on his side, the arithmetic isn't. Work today would put him fifty cents closer to buying that dress for his daughter, Dorothy, and the lady at Scholes Mercantile said the dress would be very much in style this Christmas. Problem was, from what the guys had told him, he'd be lucky to work another dozen times before Thanksgiving, and he'd still be short. Scholes wasn't extending any more credit to miners, not when they're all up to their eyes in debt already...

"Number 27! Eastenes!"

The big, ginger Greek behind Eastenes gives him a nudge. Eastenes looks around stupid.

"Last time, number 27! John Eastenes!"

Eastenes raises a hand. "Right here, Foreman!"

The mine Foreman sticks his thumb toward the cage, that creaking freight elevator that lowers the miners into the shaft. Eastenes straightens his hard hat and walks forward. Who needs arithmetic, anyway?

"Thank you, Sir!" he says to the Foreman. "I really needed this one, I'm buying my little girl a new dress-"

"Get in the cage, will ya?" says the Foreman. "And get yer hearing checked. That's the last time I call your name three times."

The Foreman drums his fingers on his clipboard. Every year, he thinks, these miner's names get stranger.

"Number 41! Rene Jacques!"

A hand raises up from the line. *"Oui, monsieur!"*

Rene Jacques steps forward, swinging his breast-auger and lunch bucket. The auger's drill bit alone is almost as tall as Jacques himself, and both items still have the initials of Jacques' brother Frank etched into them. Even the metal auger has worn smooth where Jacques has touched it. He remembers the Fire Boss in Louisville, handing the tools over the day after his brother's funeral. If he showed up for work the next day, he could have them. For half-off, of course.

The tall Greek behind Jacques watches the little Frenchman walk off, rolls his eyes, and drops his tools to the ground.

"Hey! Foreman!"

The Foreman shakes his head. "I said Jacques, not Spanudakhis."

Jacques takes his spot next to Eastenes in front of the cage door. They hear the clanking and whirring of the motors, carrying the cage back to the surface. He gives Eastenes a nod, they'd shoveled coal together before, he was a family man, trustworthy.

Back in the work line, Spanudakhis takes a step ahead, and the temperature of the line rises one degree. It was dangerous to hold up the process. All eyes are converging on him.

"Foreman, the mines closed for the summer. I just spent the last of the savings. With winter coming up, and all, well, how do I say it? I gotta work!"

The Foreman looks up from his clipboard to see the six-foot-three Greek walking toward him. "If we call your name, you'll work today" he says, "and for the record, you worked last week."

"Yeah, but six credits a week just ain't cuttin' it!"

There were rumors that the foreman had been an enforcer down in the Creede casinos, and could kill a man six ways at any moment. They said he sharpened the sides of his clipboard, slicing a miner's throat before he could knock the Foreman over and run off with the office cash box. So when the Foreman flips the clipboard over, holding it within one inch of the Greek's jugular vein, everyone holds their breath.

"You think this is some Mother Cabrini charity, Nick? If I can get you work, *I'll get you work!*"

The Foreman lowers his clipboard and pulls out a pen, ready to cross the name 'Spanudakhis' off the list. "Now get back in line. Or not."

For a second, Spanudakhis thinks about leaving. The boarding house back in Lafayette is a good six miles away, but he could make it.

Then he sees, with his mind's eye, a family, red-headed like him, running to the top of a hill beyond their small village in Crete, within the Aegean Sea. They are racing to meet the mailman, his sack of letters hauled by a donkey, each letter telling tales of life in America. What would his letter say?

Spanudakhis heads for the back of the line. On his way back, he feels the glare of every other miner, for wasting their time, and when he reaches the back, he sees something: a woman, standing at the front gate of the mine camp. Just my luck, thinks Spanudakhis. A woman at the mine.

The Foreman returns to his captive audience, and says, "We can use two more people today."

The crowd stands alert, wondering how desperate they'll need to be.

"The coal seam on level three has been more productive than we expected. You'll be moving an extra coal cart... with the old mule."

The crowd groans, curses and minced oaths from every tongue from every corner of the earth. A young man steps forward, even amongst the slight Croats and Mexicans, he seems tiny.

"Pepe, *that* old mule?" says the young man. "It won't let anyone near it!"

Jacques has heard the commotion, and hollers back at the line. "*Mise en garde, copain*, my brother died by one of those mules. Shame on you, Foreman, risking our lives with that beast!"

"It's an extra half-credit per day," says the Foreman. He points his clipboard at the young man. "You're Jerry Davis, right? The rookie. You take this shift, you might not be a rookie no more."

Davis grimaces, at twenty-one, his teeth are already graying from the chewing tobacco. It's the only thing that keeps him alert through the twelve-hour shifts, and the only thing that will let him fall asleep afterwards.

"I worked a shift with Pepe last week. The monster can barely pull a cart, it's so old." The other miners nod, and Davis adds, "Get a new mule, you cheapskates!"

"Buy a new mule?" says the Foreman. "You're crazy." The Foreman sighs. "All right. Three-quarters extra credit."

Davis hears heavy footfalls behind him, and sees Spanudakhis lumbering toward the cage, pick, shovel, and hard hat swaying with each step. He stops next to the Foreman.

"When the old mule's heart gives out," says Spanudakhis, "and the coal cart runs over me, who will pay for the funeral?"

"Beats me," says the Foreman. "I'll read a Greek poem at your wake, at that Orthodox church you go to. How about that? The cage will be back up soon."

Spanudakhis moves on. There were thousands of Greek miners out on these plains, but no Greek Orthodox churches.

The foreman watches the Greek head for the cage, smiles. Everyone has a price. Davis, the rookie, calls after him. "You're a bigger man than me. Or maybe just dumber. I'll try the next shift, maybe the mule will have keeled over and died by then."

The Foreman heads for the office, and that was that. They'd found their work for the day. Anyone who attempted an appeal by knocking on that door risked a swift strike to the teeth for trespassing. Employment at a mine was no guarantee of consistent work there. The remaining miners head back to their cottages inside the mine camp, or back to the nearest town, or head on to the State Mine a mile north.

The Columbine Mine is the crown jewel of the Rocky Mountain Fuel Company, the second-largest coal outfit in the state. Located far from other cities, the company had built its own. Within the Columbine Mine's perimeter fence was a complete city, with tenement housing, a post office, a schoolhouse, a church, a mess hall, a gambling den, and a house dedicated to the world's oldest profession. The mine even printed its own money, called scrip, which could only be spent at a store owned by the mine. Coal mines shut down during the summer months, when no-one needed to heat their homes, so a miner came back to work in the autumn with mountainous debt, pushing down like a blacksmith's anvil on his back.

The debt began the moment a miner set foot on company property. Immigrants came to America from all over the world, and they came with little money. A coal miner needs tools, which were not given but sold. Since they had no money, the price of the tools was deducted from their first paycheck. They needed a place to stay, so they usually rented a company house, of four plywood walls and a tin roof. This too was deducted from their pay, as was the food they needed to survive, and the liquor that looked more and more appealing the longer they worked. If a miner ever managed to pay off these debts, he was paid in the scrip, which became worthless scraps of paper outside of the Columbine's gate. It prevented a miner from ever saving up real money, in case he wanted to leave. When the miners lined up on pay day, looking out past the perimeter fence, the world beyond the Columbine felt a thousand miles more distant than the vast oceans they had crossed on their way here.

Spanudakhis joins Jacques and Eastenes at the cage door. Jacques has his hands clasped together, looking toward heaven.

"Brother, I miss you every day," says Jacques, "but I'm not quite ready to join you yet. Keep us safe today."

Spanudakhis looks up, too. "Yeah, what the Frog here said."

They stare ahead at the door. The shaft at the Columbine goes down hundreds of feet, and is slow to the surface, bringing up eight grown men and four tons of coal.

The Greek shrugs. "Who knows?" he says, "maybe even old mules have their good days."

"Then there's hope for you yet," says Jacques.

They laugh, but not much.

Spanudakhis glances over his shoulder. The woman he saw earlier is still standing at the mine gate, and closer, even.

"Hey, who's the woman?" asks Spanudakhis.

"I don't know," says Eastenes. "I've seen her talking to Bertha before."

"It's not good to have a woman at a mine," says Spanudakhis. "Bad luck. Damn bad luck."

Jacques scoffs. "Says who? Says no-one back home in France! Hell, back home, things were so desperate, they had men, women, and children picking coal in those tunnels."

Spanudakhis pokes Jacques on the shoulder. "Says me, froggy! One time, down by Aguilar, a little girl ran into the mine, 'Daddy, you forgot your lunch bucket!' Next day, roof cave in, crippled four men. God can be cruel like that. It's bad luck, and lemme tell ya, luck's all we got most days."

Jacques raises an eyebrow. "If it were up to me, friends, it'd be nothing but women down in those mines." Eastenes stifles a laugh, running a thumb over his wedding band.

A loud *ka-chunk* almost sends the men off their feet as the cage reaches the surface and the door slides open. Eight miners step out, so thick with coal dust they look like minstrels from a movie show, brilliant white eyes piercing through dark. They leave behind a massive mine cart, brimming over with coal. The cage door closes again, the frame moving up into the mine tipple's top level, where it's tipped over (hence the name), and the coal sorted by size for delivery to homes, rail yards, or the Lafayette power plant, where it will run street lights as far off as Larimer County, sixty miles away.

One miner lets out a bad cough, and pulls out a handkerchief to wipe off his face. Layers of soot wipe away, and soon the Greek, the frog, and Eastenes (who, by that logic, would be the bohunk), begin to recognize this miner.

Spanudakhis throws his arms wide, bellowing, "And in this corner, weighing one-hundred-and-twenty-five pounds, fresh from the Columbine night shift…"

Jacques walks over. "*Sacre bleu*, it's Johnny Kid Mex!"

"Son of a-" Eastenes catches himself. "Johnny! John Ortega!"

Slow, aching hands rise from Ortega's side to lift off his hard hat. It falls to the ground, the carbide lantern hooked onto it spilling its fuel. Kid Mex is short, almost as short as Jacques, but his muscles seem ready to launch him far over the hills. He laughs, shakes his head.

"No Kid Mex here, *amigos*, just putting in a day's work." Ortega collapses against a pile of crates, stretching and wincing.

"I thought you were working dawn-to-dusk," says Spanudakhis.

"No, dusk-to-dawn," says Ortega.

"Shoot," says Jacques, "I'd take half-pay to work a coal room with Kid Mex. He always has your back."

Ortega smiles. "And I know any of you would have mine."

The bell on the cage door rings, the people underground want to send more coal up.

"What's it like down there today?" asks Eastenes. The men trade work hazards like boys trade baseball cards.

"Stay out of Room Seven," says Ortega. "The Fire Boss said it was fine for the night shift, but all night, the ceiling was cracking and groaning like a pine tree about to fall. The coal seam in Room Five is two feet off the floor-" he grits his teeth as he cracks his back, "I was picking on my side for six hours. Let someone short, *muy bajo*, do it, like him." Ortega points to Davis, over by the pleasure hut. He's trying to peek through the windows, but they're painted black.

Ortega looks around at the miners. "Are you three the only ones left to go down this shift?"

Eastenes shrugs. "What do you think this is, Kid Mex? Some..."

"Some Mother Cabrini joint?" says Ortega. "*Dios mio*. Enjoy your day, *amigos*, and *buena suerte*."

As Ortega leaves, Spanudakhis looks confused, and Jacques informs him *suerte* is what the Greeks would call *tychi*.

"Oh. 'Luck'" says Spanudakhis. "That's what I'm tellin' 'em, luck's all we got."

Ortega watches them enter the cage, the door slams shut, cables and pulleys lowering them deep into the hillside. Ortega hates falling asleep in the day, with the noon sun clawing its way through the holes in the bedroom shutters, but the night shift was the only way he could make sure he'd see his kids before his head hit the pillow. He would hug his kids on their way to the Columbine camp's schoolhouse, and his wife Mary would be boiling water over a coal fire for his morning bath. Coal miners were the untouchable caste, the filthy foreigners in their filthy camps, and yet Ortega could name not one miner who didn't bathe every single day. The job demanded it.

Ortega had noticed the woman standing by the office. Every fool wanted to take on a boxer out in the open, and Ortega had trained himself to know when someone wanted a few words. He passes his family's cottage and walks to the side of the office, where this stranger is waiting. The coal dust follows him in a low, trailing cloud, one he would be glad to be rid of sooner than later.

"Is there something I can help you with?" he asks.

"Are you John Ortega?" asks the woman.

"No disrespect, *Señora*, but who wants to know?"

"I know your wife, Mary," she says. "She told me you're new here."

"We moved up from Pueblo last year. Came to find work."

He watches a few miners come out of the camp's general store. No work for them today, and now in more debt, but when they pass by Ortega, their faces brighten.

"The other miners seem to think well of you," says the woman.

"I used to box," says Ortega.

"And since your face is still together," says the woman, "not a bad boxer, I guess."

"Featherweight champion of the Rockies," says Ortega.

The woman gives a polite nod, and Ortega wonders what her angle is. Over in Lafayette, the old men who went to the Templo de el

Cordero used to call the town's founder *El Madre*, the Mother, firm but generous. The woman before him has that same quality.

The woman speaks. "We heard the miners in the southern counties are going on strike."

Ortega was afraid that's what this was about. *"Si,"* he says.

"Three thousand on strike, so far," says the woman. "It might come up north, too, and with winter on the way, it's going to get tight, and fast. We'll need to ration out food and clothing, and with your popularity amongst the miners, I'd like to know if we can have you on our team."

Ortega sighs. *"Señora..."*

"Beranek," says the woman.

"Mrs. Beranek, *por favor*, there is a reason I did not stay in the Southern Coal Field. I came here to work. I have four children of my own."

"Oh," says Beranek, "I see..." She looks down at the mud. A bad idea, this was.

"But, if I cannot work," says Ortega, "I can help others. *"Somos todos hijos de Dios. Ayudamos mutamente.* I have family in the mining camps around here. Perhaps I can get them to help with... food and clothing?"

Beranek smiles. "That would be wonderful. Your wife said you were a good man. Partners then, Mister Ortega?"

She extends a hand. Ortega looks back at the dark tipple of the Columbine Mine, shrugs, and gives her hand a vigorous shake. Clouds of coal dust fly off his clothes and onto Beranek's. When he lets go, Beranek forces a grin, and as she turns away, she reaches for a handkerchief of her own.

Ortega chuckles. "A retired boxer and a housewife. A coupla regular charity tycoons like Rockefeller, *si*?"

"A team-up for the ages," says Beranek.

"Do you have any children, Mrs. Beranek?" asks Ortega.

"Yes," she says, "sixteen."

"Oh, then he's old enough to work at-" Ortega stops. "Wait, you have one child who's sixteen, or you've... *made*..." Ortega is counting on his fingers, his eyes growing wide.

Beranek cranes her neck to make eye contact. "Are you all right, Mister Ortega?"

Ortega sighs. "Yes, it's just... I thought ten rounds in the ring took stamina, but, *ay mio*, you may have me beat!"

"We're tough folk in the Northern Coal Field," says Beranek, "Do try to keep up."

Ortega watches Beranek leave though the front gate, and heads back to his family's cottage for bath and bed.

CHAPTER TWO

Your Local Wobbly

Gorden's Grocery in Lafayette keeps a truck idling on the curb for deliveries on the half-hour. Two street musicians are leaning forward on the truck, their hands pressed against the warm engine. Cold October nights turn a guitar player's hands into gnarled meat hooks, so the engine keeps them ready until a paying customer walks by.

The day shift has ended, the mines of the coal field have blown their whistles. Most miners at the Columbine, like John Ortega, live in the mine camp's company housing, though a great many come home to the neighboring cities of Lafayette, Louisville, and Erie. In Lafayette, miners had a shot at owning their own homes, although the Rocky Mountain Fuel Company still operated a scrip-only company store along Simpson Street, in addition to the one in the Columbine Camp.

Most of the miners have made their way up Simpson Street already, stopping at the stores for last-minute supplies. Wives purchased groceries on a daily basis. Farther up Simpson, a pack of farmhands from the east side of town are hitching their horses at the Jewel Theatre, to catch the late movie. Children kick up clouds of dirt from the unpaved road, diving behind telephone poles, firing make-believe guns in games of Cowboys and Indians that their fathers and grandfathers had played for real. Tiny cottages, bookending the business district, are alight with soft scarlet and orange as the dinner fires die down. Inside the mercantile store, the clerk reads a copy of the *Lafayette Leader* with his feet on the counter. His eyes scan over the weekly Christian Science column, offering the latest research on which prayers will cure which diseases. As the crowds thin out, and the children return home, the hum of the electric streetlights, and nickering horses, fill the quiet spaces of the street, and the two musicians spot a trio of prospects coming up the road.

The trio come closer to the musicians, stopping under the streetlights at Michigan Avenue, groaning, shuffling in a kind of askew crab-walk. This crab-walk is the universal identifier of a miner, they acquired it from picking and shoveling on their backs for hour upon hour. From the Michigan intersection, Simpson Street begins its slow incline to meet Public Road to the east. The feeblest horse in the nearby livery stable could handle that hill, but it stops Jacques, Eastenes, and Spanudakhis dead in their tracks.

Jacques looks up at Spanudakhis. "You know something, Greek?"

"What's that, Jay-coo?"

"It's terrifying to see your life flash before your eyes, but the seventh or eighth time, it gets a little old.'"

Eastenes nods, and wheezes out, "I'd like to ask God to show me someone else's life next time."

They hear the bell ring on the company store's door. It's Davis, carrying a bag of raw pinto. "Whaddaya know, who let these brutes out?"

"Whaddaya know?" says Jacques.

For a moment, Simpson Street bounces with that standard miner's greeting of "Whaddaya know," applicable in any and all situations a coal-digger might find themselves in.

"Night shift?" asks Eastenes.

Davis nods. "Anything I should know about tonight?"

Spanudakhis grunts. "What shouldn't you know? That's a shorter list."

Eastenes hears tiny footfalls behind him, and knows who it is. He just wanted a few more minutes to prepare himself, before he sprang his day onto his family.

"Daddy!" yells Dorothy. Dorothy grew every time he saw her. Eastenes picks his daughter up, swinging her around, her hair ribbons pulled far to the right. He sees his wife Bertha walking up, too. She knows, with that ESP some spouses share, that something went wrong today. He hates laying his worries on Bertha, her days are just as hard.

"And just what are you doing out of bed?" Eastenes asks Dorothy.

"You didn't give us your pie yet!" she says.

Uh-oh, thinks Eastenes. The pie. Every coal miner in America carries a lunch bucket. The lower half is a pail for water (more often filled with beer), and the top part carries a sandwich and a slice of pie. No matter if the miner had three children, or ten, half the pie was divided amongst the children. Even if the coal companies made him work a 20-hour shift, Eastenes was sure he would still come home to find his children's eyes peeking at him through the cottage shutters, waiting for that pie.

"A pie like this is a special occasion," says Eastenes. "Table settings, cinnamon sprinkles, and milk! How about you run back home and get it ready?" Dorothy runs back home without a word, sure to relay the message to her five brothers and sisters. As soon as she's out of earshot, Eastenes turns to Spanudakhis, and says, "Do you have any spare credits? I need to get another slice of pie."

"Now hold on," says Bertha. "You only eat the whole pie when you get nervous. What happened this time?"

"His support beam rotted out," blurts the Greek. "The whole damn roof collapsed."

Bertha draws in her breath, readying a cry of exasperation, but she doesn't have it in her tonight. While she'll never know the mad scramble out of a coal room as the rock crushed everything left behind to splinters, she is well-acquainted with the sound of three blasts from the mine whistle, meaning something terrible had happened, and the dread of wondering if death had come for her family this time.

She grabs her husband, hugging him close. "To beat hell, not again!" she says. "If they'd just pay you to put up a new beam, is that too much to ask?"

Bertha walks up the street, and looks back at Eastenes while walking backwards. "And try not to break your neck on the way home!" she yells, "If you get hurt, I'll kill you!" She ignores the snickering of the street musicians.

"Nice to see you too, dear," says Eastenes, and, turning back to the other miners, says, "Almost broke my leg getting out of that room when it caved in."

"Ah, that rotted beam's been on its way out for weeks," says Davis. "Why didn't you replace it, East?"

"It would have been deducted from my pay, rookie!" says Eastenes. "We need that money for heating. Dorothy got pneumonia last year, I'm not risking that again."

Jacques smirks and says, "Or maybe the heating money fell down a beer bottle."

Far be it, thinks Eastenes, for a Louisville Frenchman to suggest that. Over in the Frenchtown district, miners were known for their homemade wine, sold by the barrel in the speakeasies of Front Street.

"Believe me, *mon-sewer* Jay-coo," says Eastenes, "some days I wish it had, but in Lafayette, if you get caught with booze, they can take away your house! It's written right into the deed." He grumbles something about 'uptight Methodists', and raises a holy hand to the waning crescent moon. "So praise be, my immortal soul is unmolested by the devil's drink, *hallelujah*!"

"Funny, isn't it?" says a voice behind them.

The four of them turn to see an old, gangly man standing by the livery stable. Jacques knows him, and thinks that for a man who couldn't shut up once he got going, Bell was very light on his feet. He was older than most miners, with wise eyes guarded behind spectacles. Davis had worked a coal room once with him, he'd said he was new in town. As an outsider, he had erred on the side of caution, assimilating with the locals, but not too much. As he steps under the streetlight, they see he's carrying his ever-present book of local laws and statutes.

"What's funny?" asks Eastenes. He still feels an acid taste in his mouth from Jacques' question.

Bell smiles. "We work all day, digging coal by carbide light, dodging rock and rotten wood beams, until we'd give our right arm for enough liquor to take the pain away. Keep us from realizing it doesn't have to be like that."

"Oh, not you again" says Jacques.

"Who, again?" asks Eastenes.

The old man extends a hand to Eastenes. "Adam Bell. Your local Wobbly."

"Wobbly?" asks Eastenes.

"Wobbly," repeats Bell, "A representative of the Industrial Workers of the World."

"A *union*" whispers Jacques.

"Oh..." says Eastenes, thinking for a moment. "So why do they call you a Wobbly?"

Bell shrugs. "No-one knows. One day it just stuck."

Eastenes is confused.

Jacques prods Bell's shoulder. "Hey, there's not really a strike down south, right?"

"More and more people joining every day," says Bell.

"Great," says Jacques. He pulls out his box of chewing tobacco and bites off a corner before passing it over to Davis. "Just what we need. Everyone out of work, right before winter."

"Marooned in a frozen wasteland," says Davis. He gnaws at the tobacco, forming a thick, wet coat of brown in his mouth.

"No-one to feed our wives and children," says Eastenes.

"Not a happy thought," says Bell, "no argument there, comrade."

"Well, count me out, pal," says Eastenes. "My family needs a strike like I need two left feet."

"Remember the last strike? The Long Strike?" says Jacques, "Five years we held out, five years! For nothing!"

"There was a lady in Lafayette," says Eastenes. "Mary Miller. She founded this town, and ran the bank. She loaned money to miners during the strike, kept them from starving. The miners lived, but her bank was ruined."

"Then," says Jacques, "people started dying."

The men named off the violence they had seen or heard of. The Lafayette police chief torn apart by a mob. The strikebreaker in Superior, who died in a shootout with police at the train depot. The guards at the Hecla in Louisville, who tried to stop a siege of the mine by drowning the strikers with a flooded reservoir.

In a low whisper, Eastenes adds one word:

"Ludlow."

The word hangs in the air like a cloud of smoke.

Eastenes looks at Bell. "I hear the old miners talk about Ludlow. The White City. The coal company thugs killed nineteen people."

The month of April hung heavy in the minds of coal miners, because April had been the month of Ludlow. After four life-draining years of strike, strikers in the southern coal field had built a tent colony at Ludlow, two hundred miles south of Lafayette. Guards had made sport of firing their guns into the tents, the homes they called the White City, and so miners had dug deep trenches underneath for their families to hide in. On April 20th, 1914, the guards set fire to the tents, and as the flames spread, wives and children, crowded in those trenches, suffocated on the smoke.

The miners had asked for fair pay. They asked for the mines to be safe. Since they were paid by the ton for the coal they mined, they asked for weigh machines that actually worked. For all this, the coal companies opted to wait it out, until that day in April when the White City was devoured by flame, when all watched wives, sons, and daughters die cowering in their own graves. It had been thirteen years since Ludlow, and not one coal miner could say his life had improved. April hung heavy for a miner, indeed, for it was the grief of Good Friday, without the redemption of Easter. When a miner thought of Ludlow, his blood ran as black as the coal.

"We can't have another Ludlow, Mister Bell," says Eastenes. Davis and Jacques chew faster.

Bell stares down at his scuffed shoes. "I had friends at Ludlow, mister. Not a day goes by that I don't think of them. I guess if we don't strike, that can't ever happen again."

Jacques applauds. "See, even a stupid Wobbly can learn!"

"We can expect the same old thing, over and over," says Bell. "More rotten wood beams, because they still won't pay you to put up new ones. And when they do pay you, they can pay you with scrip, that fake money the Columbine prints, that can only be spent at a store they own. That way, you can never save up enough money to leave. That's what we can look forward to if we don't strike: more of the same. Tell me, Mister..." Bell points at the Greek.

"Spanudakhis."

"Mister Spanudakhis, when was the last time you saw the sun?"

"Well, let's see..." Spanudakhis counts on his fingers, mouthing out the numbers.

"Last Sunday, I bet," says Bell. "You go into the mine before the sun is up, and when the steam whistle blows, and you come back up, the sun has already set. For a coal miner, Sunday really is a 'sun-day.'"

Davis speaks up, "Say, wasn't there a song like that, in Louisville?"

"*Oui,*" says Jacques, "it's *Nuit Charboneuesse*, no?"

"*Charbon*, that's 'coal', I think" says Davis. "I heard it as *Coal-Black Night*."

Jacques yells over to the street musicians by Gorden's Grocery. "Hey! You two! Play us that song *Nuit Charboneuesse*!"

The two musicians look at each other. With hardly a beat, their fingers pluck across the strings, playing those twangy, high-lonesome melodies that carry through every coal town from the Book Cliffs of Utah to the grasslands of Oklahoma.

Jacques had called it *Nuit Charboneuesse*, and others called it *Coal-Black Night*, but the story of the song was the same in all tongues. On a cold winter morning, a young boy followed the wagon trails out of town to a frozen lake. Out on the far shore, the windows of the power plant cast a sunset glow over the ice. The boy saw a group of old men standing on the lake shore, playing bocce ball, taking sips of company-store whiskey. The boy asked the old men if he could play with them, and one of them, annoyed, told the boy to go home.

The boy did go home, and his mother asked him why he was crying. The boy said "that man" sent him home. What man, asked his mother. "The man I see on Sundays," he said.

The mother said, *"Don't worry, child, I know the one. That was your father, and you're his son."*

The last chord of the song hangs suspended in the air on Simpson Street. Eastenes looks up to see the first wisps of snow descend on the town. The flakes swoop low, dancing a few inches off the ground, before pooling into dark blotches in the dirt road.

Winter was not far away, and in the story of the song, the men saw the future all too clear. The pain of Ludlow had resigned them to a world where men forgot their children's faces, and children never saw their fathers. They believed they'd be paid next week, or believed they would have another drink, but that was about all they did believe.

In the quiet snowfall, the years since Ludlow stretched long behind them. They knew what that road felt like. Could they survive that same road, for another thirteen years? How did the song go, again? "Sold my body away for a dollar a day, now you got my spirit for free."

"Hey Nick."

Spanudakhis looks over at Eastenes.

"See if they have any pies left at the company store. My little girl wants some dessert with her dad."

The men go their separate ways. Bell hopes the boarding house didn't lock him out again. He feels Eastenes still watching him, and looks back.

"Mister Bell?" says Eastenes. "I hope you know what you're doing. Count us in."

The snow is falling harder as the men hurry home.

CHAPTER THREE

Rudy the Mule

On October 21st, the newsmen in Boulder were focused on a concert by superstar and patriot extraordinaire John Philip Sousa, and news that miners had voted to bring the strike up to the northern counties had gone ignored. By the middle of November, three weeks later, it could be ignored no longer. The long lines of miners who had commuted to the Columbine were now replaced by even greater crowds, making their way along the highway out of Lafayette, up the county line road, to picket at the mine's perimeter fence.

Amidst the chants of Solidarity, Elizabeth Beranek marches to the front of the picket line with a towering pile of blankets.

"Everyone listen up! I've got blankets from the church. Everyone chipped in to get you these, so take one, and I don't want to hear a whimper or whine that they're too thin. The way these strikes go, it might be over before lunch today, so at least you got a free blanket out of it."

"Over before lunch?" cries Davis. "I was up all night, working on this sign!"

Beranek looks at Davis' hand-drawn signboard, an arched black cat hissing at her, universal pictogram of the Wobblies.

She shrugs, and tells Davis, "Use it to scare rats away."

Adam Bell hops off his improvised pulpit, an empty dynamite box. "That's what we're here to do, Mrs. Beranek, only the rats I'm after sleep in mansions, and eat off fine china."

Beranek rolls her eyes. "Mister Bell, you can parade with Trotsky later. For now..." Beranek throws the blanket pile at Bell with a hearty *fwoomf*, "you can help hand out supplies."

Jacques, Ortega, and Spanudakhis arrive at the gate, dressed, like everyone else, in fresh-pressed shirts and jackets. Miners spend six days a week covered in grease and soot. Their clothes were ragged, torn, with boots held together by belts. Their wives worked on their hands and knees, scrubbing floors and washing dishes. To be able to wear a suit on Sunday was a blessing.

There was another reason, of course. Every miner knew their next day of work could be the one where the roof caves in, the dynamite misfires, an enraged mule shatters their ribs, or the cage's cable snaps, sending them plummeting down into the abyss. Their wives would hear that terrible sound, of three short blasts from the mine whistle. A miner needed a fresh suit at all times, since it might be the suit he got buried in. For this reason, all laundry was done on a Monday.

"Another excellent church service," says Jacques.

"Not bad," says Spanudakhis, "for a Catholic ceremony. Someday I must invite you all to an Orthodox service."

"Perhaps, my Greek friend," says Jacques.

Ortega says nothing, but inhales the crisp air and flexes his arms. The air seemed fresher now, with the mines shut down. From the Columbine Mine, the hills descend to the county line road, up to the hills of Lafayette, and back down to the great Boulder Valley, where all of a sudden the high peaks of the Rocky Mountains rise up, white and violet in the distance. All across the valley, and in the Carbon Valley to the north, were coal mines his *familia* worked at. One by one, the miners had begun to say "enough," demanding honest pay and safety. Ortega had learned early on, as a boy in Pueblo, that a bully will take you for everything he can, unless you stand up and are ready to fight. It felt good to make a stand again.

Bell, the old Wobbly, had said it best when he talked about the mine owners, sitting in their private clubs, clinking glasses of scotch, and charting out the courses of their businesses. Why was it, asked Bell, that it was okay for them to talk amongst themselves, and make plans, but them guys digging the coal couldn't talk or make plans? Why did that get you thrown in jail as an agitator?

"Yes, a good service" says Eastenes, remembering the morning's sermons and liturgies, "All good except for Bell over here, trying to debate the priest!"

Bell tosses his last blanket to a picketer, fixing his glasses. "I'm telling you, read the Bible! Here we have a union carpenter..."

"Not again," moans Jacques.

Bell continues, "... A man who preached compassion for all men. *'Blessed are ye poor, for yours is the Kingdom of Heaven!' 'Woe unto you that is rich, for you have received your consolation!'* The evidence is clear, comrades, Jesus was a socialist."

Spanudakhis puts a giant hand on Bell's shoulder, Bell looks up at the tall Greek.

"Mister Bell, you are a good man, and I am proud to picket with you, but that is the stupidest thing I have ever heard."

Bell changes the subject. "I've heard good news from Walsenburg, in the southern counties. Twelve thousand miners on strike so far."

Jacques says, "Maybe the mine owners will give us a fair shake this time."

"As usual," says Bell, "The state's coming down hard. The police are raiding union halls. I heard they even arrested Flaming Mamie and her sister, at a march up Delagua Canyon."

"Flaming Mamie?" asks Spanudakhis.

"She's a new recruit in the Wobbly cause," says Bell. "Nineteen years old, with a passion for justice and the working man like we've never seen! When police came to put down the protests, she held her ground against men twice her size!" Bell puts a hand to his bosom, and closes his eyes, swooning. "She's been stirring up absolute hell down south, a woman after my own heart!"

Bell opens his eyes to find himself face-to-face with a mule. Bell bolts back, and the men laugh as the Foreman leads the mule away.

"I see the Foreman has a special someone in his life," says Eastenes.

The Foreman gives the mule's rope a tug. "Get away from 'em, Rudy," he growls to the mule, "I don't need you gettin' ideas about class warfare or nothin'."

"If it isn't Rudy, whaddaya know?" exclaims Jacques. He slaps the mule's flank, the mule responds with a squawk. "What's he doing out of the mine?"

"One of his shoes came loose," says the Foreman. "I'm sending him down with the next cage."

Mules lived in special stables, far down in the mines. They usually came up for the summer months, when the mines were closed, to go work on the farms. To see a mule in the daylight in winter was like seeing a kangaroo on Pikes Peak.

The Foreman swings an arm at the men, shooing them away. "And get back outside the gate!" he barks, "Hard enough running a mine without you worthless freeloaders mucking about!"

"You think striking is easy, *jefe*," says Ortega, "try it sometime."

"Or pay us a wage we can live on," says Bell, "Or dare I say, pay us with actual money, not this scrip you shamefully peddle."

The crowd of picketers applauds, and when Rudy the mule rears his head, letting out a *hee-yaw*, the applause turns to roars of laughter. The Foreman's face flushes fire-engine red, and he ties the mule to a hitching post outside his office, gritting his teeth as he pulls the last knot tight.

"You want wages?" shouts the Foreman. "Here's a week's advance!" The foreman produces a gesture most inappropriate for a Sunday morning, stomps into the office, and slams the door.

The men look on at the mule, half-blind and aloof to the plight of the miners. The miners invariably came to respect the mules, and viewed them as companions in the daily underground struggle of life and death. Even Jacques, whose own brother was kicked to death by one, could name every mule at the Columbine, their strengths and weaknesses, and whether they preferred oats or vegetables.

"Just think, *amigos*," says Ortega, "Rudy lives down in that mine, away from the wind and rain, cool in the summer, warm in the winter."

"Three square meals a day," says Eastenes.

"I wish the mine paid for my food," says Jacques. "The Blue Parrot in Louisville won't let you pay with scrip."

It was a rich wellspring of gallows humor for the men, that the mules really did have the better end of the deal. A mule had lodging, food, medical care, and equipment all paid for by the mine. A miner had to get all of these things for himself, and if he quit, got sick, or died, there were a hundred hungry miners ready to replace him. Breeding a mule, and raising it to working age, represented an enormous investment on the part of the mine.

Ortega had told his friends a story about a mine down by Trinidad. The foreman there had felt the ground shake, heard the steam whistle blow three times. The tunnels had been ripped apart in an explosion. Dozens of lives snuffed out in an instant, wives widowed, children thrust off into orphanages since there was now no money to raise them. The foreman sprinted into the office, horror and tears in his eyes, and cried out, "How many mules were killed?"

They had howled like wild dogs when Ortega first told that story, the same laughter and macabre fraternity perhaps shared by death row inmates, or soldiers in combat.

According to Bell's trusty law book, it was illegal in Colorado to kill or mistreat a mule. The miner who did that was sure to never work again. Moreover, it was illegal for a miner to even complain in public about his working conditions. Bell knew all too well that to stand on a soap box, armed only with your voice and ideas, was too great a threat to the state, and the companies that owned it. To protest in public was to risk a month in the local jail, the first night spent blinded by the blood oozing from your scalp.

Yes, the men had decided that no-one had it better than a mule. Bell, Ortega, Jacques and Eastenes are laughing about it, marveling at the absurdity of it all, when the bags come down over their heads, dragged by the neck into a black van that speeds away before anyone can notice they're gone.

CHAPTER FOUR

Invasive, Foreign Parasites

Eastenes feels his body thrown from the back of the van, landing in hard dirt. Wind whistles beneath the bag, a dull light is all he can see. He's pulled to his feet, pushed forward by something hard, and he hears dry grass crackle beneath his feet until a gruff voice cuts through:

"That's far enough."

Eastenes stops, behind him comes the *snik* of a pocketknife opening. His blood runs cold for a second, and then he feels the rope binding his hands back come loose. He lifts his arms up, and pulls the bag off his face, blinking away the harsh sunlight, until he sees Ortega, Bell, and Jacques in front of him, doing the same. Eastenes spins around, first taking in the grassland extending far to the horizon, and then the uniformed men with guns standing behind them. The shortest and squattest of them, also the one with the shiniest badge, holds his revolver out at hip-height. It seems tiny in his fat hands.

Bell squints through his glasses, smiles in recognition. "Sheriff Ben Robinson! How's the gout?"

"You're washed up, Adam," says the Sheriff.

Eastenes' eyes turn westward, and he stares, mouth-open, at the shimmering white shapes peeking just above the horizon line. "Is them... is them the Rockies? How far have you taken us?"

Robinson pushes his revolver into its holster, and raises a big, round finger to the east. "Kansas is a three hour's walk that way. I suggest you get moving."

Eastenes looks over to Bell, eyes wide with panic. "Bell, what's going on?"

"We've been 'white-capped', John," says Bell, pointing at the distant, snow-tipped summits. "A free trip to the state line, courtesy of our local law enforcement."

Robinson grunts. "And a free trip to jail if you come back."

Ortega kicks up a cloud of dirt. "*Hijas de putas*, you kidnap us from our families!"

"Shut up!" snaps Robinson. "I won't let a bunch of socialist, anarchist, communist agitators threaten the safety of Weld County. Go ahead, Bell, call it tyranny, call it a violation of your rights. If you ask me, the only time I hear someone invoke their rights is when I'm slappin' the cuffs on 'em."

Bell ignores the bait. "Are you familiar with the Hastings Mine, Sheriff?"

"What of it?"

"Ten years ago," says Bell, "the Hastings Mine, near Ludlow, had to blow the three whistles. One hundred and twenty-one men killed in an explosion. Basic safety regulations, the kind most other mining districts see as routine, would have prevented it."

Sheriff Robinson leans back and raises an eyebrow for his deputies, they smirk back.

"Hey!" yells Eastenes. "I pray every night I'll come back to Bertha and my little ones in one piece, and they do the same for me. But I'm starting to think that just doing my job shouldn't require the Lord's constant oversight!"

"That's all we're asking for," says Bell. "Not champagne in our bucket, not caviar in the mess hall, just some peace of mind, a living wage, and a union, so we can bring our concerns to the companies."

"You know what I see?" growls the Sheriff. "Four men with no good English, without two pennies to rub together, who want nothing more than to drink, gamble, whore, and fill the streets with your screaming brats. And on top of it, you want us to foot the bill for ya!" The Sheriff snorts and spits, and a long strand of snot dangles from a stalk of prairie grass, oozing its way over a mantis cocoon. "Socialists!" he hollers. "Malcontents! Provocators!"

Bell rubs his glasses on his shirt, and says, "Actually, Sheriff, it's *provocateurs*."

The Sheriff balls his hands into fists. "Bell, if I hear one more word come out of your mouth..."

"Now wait just a minute!" says Jacques. "You think I left my life and land behind because I hate America? One of my buddies, Mike Vidovitch, he's sure a foreigner, but he signed up to fight the Kaiser before anyone else in Erie! My big brother Frank, he fought in the Great War, too!"

The Sheriff laughs. "Your brother fought in the Great War, ha! Probably some plea deal to avoid jail for a drunken brawl!"

Jacques raises a fist, French curses streaming from his mouth. In an instant, the deputies' hands have dropped to their holsters. Bell, old but fast for his age, leaps between the factions, one hand extended to either side.

"Enough!" shouts the Wobbly. "It's not worth it, Jay-coo. I'm sorry, Sheriff, our French comrade here forgets the Wobblies are a non-violent union. We fight with ideas and reason. You might try it sometime, Sheriff."

"You know what I call that?" says the Sheriff. *"Caca... de vaca!"*

* * * *

At that very moment, two hundred miles away in Boulder, at the foot of the Rockies, a man sits in front of a typewriter, chomping on a cigar. His fingers beat a staccato rhythm on the typewriter, and his eyes gleam at the words are struck onto the page.

The door opens, and Lucius Carver Paddock, editor-in-chief of the *Boulder Daily Camera*, doesn't even look up from his writing. "Yes?"

"Mister Paddock, you have a phone call from CF&I."

Paddock stops typing, and his teeth work the cigar from one side of his mouth to the other, thinking.

"Tell them I'm very busy at the moment. When they insist a second time, send it through to my office." He yanks a finished page away from the typewriter platen, and rolls in a fresh one.

A half-minute later, the phone rings, and Paddock picks up the receiver.

"*Boulder Daily Camera*, editor speaking."

Paddock recognizes the voice on the other end, razor-sharp, cool, as measured as pharmacist's medicine. "Good morning, Mister Paddock."

Paddock leans back in his chair. "Well if it isn't Mister Welburn, Rockefeller's right-hand-man in the Pueblo-land!"

"That's *Well-born*, Mister Paddock."

"My mistake," says Paddock. "How goes things in the Southern Coal Fields, sir?"

On the other end of the telephone, Welborn takes a sip of whiskey (neat). He looks out on the concrete canyons of Denver from his office in the Boston Building, nine stories of modern, sensible architecture crafted in hellfire-red stone.

"Let me see... we've got twelve thousand miners on strike, and counting, various divisions of management wanting my head, so how do you think it's going?"

Back in Boulder, Paddock pulls the cigar out of his mouth. "Well I think this strike is outrageous! Seditious! Subversive! Incendiary! Treasonous! And it's *rude*, too!"

"Mister Paddock," says Welborn, "I've been asked by Mister Rockefeller himself to rectify this... problem. I speak with the Governor this afternoon, but we need to be sure we can count on the regional press. What do you say to a new ad campaign in your paper, about the dangers posed by radical foreign agents to the state coal industry? Daily, full-page ads, of course."

Paddock leans back, computing the numbers in his head. "Daily, full-page ads, you say?" His journalist instincts had been correct: there was a huge story breaking across the state's coal fields, and this sweet, juicy offer proved it.

Paddock leans forward again. "Mister Welborn, I always appreciate the support of our faithful advertisers, but I'm afraid your money's no good here. You see, I run radical foreign agents out of town for free. These pathetic picketers pose a great peril to our very way of life. The full force of our editorial section will be wielded against these invasive, foreign parasites, and this rebellion they call a 'strike.'"

Back in Denver, Welborn takes another sip of whiskey. His faith in an impartial press, conscious of industry concerns, has not been misplaced.

"Much obliged, Mister Paddock," says Welborn. "I salute a fellow captain of industry." He puts the receiver back on its hook, pleased to have saved his stockholders the expense of buying up a newspaper.

Ten minutes later, Welborn is in his Packard limousine, headed for the State Capitol. What a complete and utter mess this has been, he thinks.

Down at his company's steel mill in Pueblo, sparks rain onto the floor, and molten metal glows in titanic pools like liquid sunlight. It is Vulcan's forge, brought down from the cloud tops of Mount Olympus, to the plains of the Wild West. The Pueblo steel mill is the beating heart of a corporate leviathan that holds sway over all who live in the Centennial State: CF&I, Colorado Fuel & Iron.

Like untold multitudes, Jesse Welborn owes his job to his boss, John D. Rockefeller, a name familiar to every man, woman, and child on the continent. Rockefeller's life had leapt straight out of a Horatio Alger novel: born of modest means to an absent, con-artist father and a pious mother in the obscurities of New England, Rockefeller had built his company, Standard Oil, into the largest on Earth. Standard Oil, with its network of wells and refineries, commanded a ninety-percent market share for oil,and the modern age ran on oil. His fortune put kings and rajas to shame, with power that made presidents and premiers look like children playing checkers.

The key to Rockefeller's success was his talent for buying out a failing company and introducing it to the concept of efficiency. This is what he had done for CF&I long ago. Rockefeller had made CF&I efficient for the steelmaking business.

CF&I's main product was steel, so naturally CF&I's steel mill in Pueblo was the largest west of the Mississippi. Steelmaking requires immense heat, only a purified form of coal known as 'coke' burned hot enough. So CF&I

owned the ovens necessary to turn coal into coke, and the surrounding town of Cokedale, where the coke-oven laborers lived. The coal to make coke came from CF&I mines, with laborers who worked at towns CF&I owned, paid with scrip CF&I issued, which could only be used at stores CF&I owned. True, their main business was steel, but they owned half of the coal mines in Colorado (or 52%, Welborn would clarify).

Steelmaking also requires limestone, supplied by CF&I's limestone quarries. Vast quantities of water were required to cool the molten metal. This water was obtained from a network of reservoirs in CF&I's possession. With the exception of a single ditch in the San Luis Valley, across the mountains from Pueblo, Colorado Fuel & Iron had a legal claim to every drop of water that fell on the state before anyone else.

And yet, for their total dominance of industry in the state, CF&I was merely a tiny piece of an even bigger corporate empire, for the purpose of all this steelmaking was to make railroad ties for the railroads Rockefeller owned, to ship his oil ocean-to-ocean, from the

Gulf of Mexico to the Great Lakes of the north. To Welborn, CF&I, in its marvelous complexity and precision, resembled a fine Swiss clock. It was efficient, and beautiful, in the way the arrangements of a symphony or a chess match can be beautiful.

This is why it disgusts Welborn to even contemplate that this intricate organization, an organization that employed a full one out of ten working laborers in Colorado, was now placed in grave danger by some ragtag strikers.

Back in the Long Strike, he'd dealt with another union, the United Mine Workers. The UMW had fought five years to make the coal companies pay attention, and were bankrupted in the process. The embarrassment of Ludlow, which had been on CF&I's ledger, had all but faded from the consumer's memory. Now, these moronic, madcap Wobblies had swept through, and done more in a month than the UMW had in half a decade.

Welborn had tried to work with the miners, Lord knows he'd tried. He was very proud of CF&I's company newspaper, the *Industrial Bulletin*, which communicated management's ideas to the workforce. For example, it helped to lay out in a column that CF&I couldn't put in an eight-hour workday unless US Steel in Pittsburgh did it first. Simple economics. It was Rockefeller's idea to create a company-owned union to hear some of the worker's concerns. That had failed, and then Welborn was blindsided by that small strike in 1919. Even sitting in the limousine, the thought of that humiliation spread scarlet across Welborn's face.

Welborn shares Rockefeller's dream to build a better world for his workers. Rockefeller workers, who read Rockefeller newspapers, whose children went to Rockefeller schools, praying in Rockefeller churches. Vaccines for diseases that had scourged humanity for so long, funded and developed by Rockefeller foundations.

Now the Wobblies are threatening that dream. They seem to feel human progress and equality are not gifts from a generous businessman, but rights, guaranteed to everyone. Yes, that was part of it, and he could not deny the feeling of being sucker-punched, once again, by the very miners who owed so much to CF&I. Welborn believes in progress and equality, he believes that corporations can be a force for good, a paternal, guiding force toward achieving progress. Sometimes, a paternal force means a firm hand.

The limousine comes to a stop, and Welborn looks out the window at the gold dome of the state capitol. The door is swung open for him at the steps, and Welborn goes over his message for the Governor once more. The strikers had come fast and hard, Welborn thinks, but so will he.

* * * *

Inside his office, Governor Billy Adams stares out at the jumbled streets and trolley lines of Denver, and the distant mountains, towering high above man's small designs. His big brother, and Governor before him, Alva Adams, had warned him, this job offers no rest. It was a nonstop run, one election to another.

Adams hears the door click open behind him. "Governor Adams" says that measured voice.

"Mister Welborn," says Adams, "please give Rockefeller my best regards, but my office is not ready to make a statement yet."

"Governor, please," says Welborn, "the situation in the coal fields is getting out of hand."

Adams steps around his desk. "When I was a private citizen, back in Alamosa, I handled all of my business matters discretely. If an employee took issue with me, or I with them, I didn't go running off to city council. I tried to act like a businessman, understand?"

"I'm afraid we're far past that now, Governor," says Welborn. "It's our employees, but they are your electorate. Are you going to tolerate your citizens chanting 'bum work for bum pay'? Jeering at co-workers who cross the picket lines? Our stockholders expect more, Governor."

Adams crosses the room to his chair, "And what are these striker's demands?"

"They want a wage of seven and a half dollars."

"Good Lord!" cries Adams. "Seven dollars an *hour*?"

"No, per day" says Welborn.

"Oh" says Adams. "That's in keeping with inflation, I believe."

"That's not all, Governor. They want us, *us*! to pay for their safety, and say they want us to be 'accountable' when we pay them for their work."

"I would say it's in a company's best interest that their employees can work a shift without injury or death."

Welborn throws his arms up. "Worst of all they want to unionize!"

"Every other mining state in the Rockies is unionized," says Adams. "They found a way to make it work." Adams watches Welborn looking out the window of the office, the same view he was contemplating a few minutes ago. "Just what is it you need from my office?"

Welborn turns back to Adams. His words carry across the office, blunt and acerbic. Adams bolts up from his chair.

"Reactivate the Rangers?" shouts Adams. "The state militia? Mister Welborn, you're out of line!"

Welborn steps away from the window. "Governor, their time has come again. If they cannot be used in a time of crisis, then when?"

Adams paces the room. "Welborn, these state militias, they never work out. Never. Glorified gunmen, from Sand Creek to Ludlow, it's like trying to cook food with dynamite shavings, you just can't control it!" Adams had heard stories from his ranching days, of cowboys who had tried cooking like that on long cattle drives. At least, he had heard what was left of them. It astounds Adams how some men thought a lot of sound and fury, guns and TNT, was the quick fix to any and all problems. How rarely that was the case.

Welborn smiles, and opens his arms, "Governor, just last year, this state was run by a bunch of white-hooded lunatics, the Ku Klux Klan." Welborn points at Adams. "You put an end to that. Where is that decisiveness now, when these Wobbly savages are banging at the door, like the Visigoths marching on Rome?"

Adams nods. "Yes, I ended the Klan's rule over our public offices. Good riddance. In doing so, I won the labor vote. When the Klan burned their crosses in someone's lawn, for being foreign or Catholic, or both, a good many of those foreigners and Catholics were coal miners. The Klan may have seen them as inferior, or unworthy, and I have no doubt there are some bad fellas amongst them. Still, those who dig our coal, or mill our steel, should have just as much a chance to be part of this nation as anybody else."

Welborn stares back at the Governor in deep concentration. Outside, they can hear the sound of a trolley releasing its air brake, and begin its slow lumbering forward. They have time to hear it gather speed on Lincoln Avenue, clang its bell, and make its slow turn onto Colfax.

The steel tycoon looks square at the Governor. "Well, Governor, since you're such a fan of the 'labor vote', I will assume you are familiar with their hero, Leon Trotsky."

"Now you listen here," says Adams.

"No," says Welborn, *"You listen*. I would assume you have read the essay where Trotsky says, 'If you cannot acquaint a man with reason, acquaint his head with the pavement.' I can see the window for reason is behind us now, Governor, so I will be as clear as I can: if we don't see some momentum on this strike matter, I will personally inform Mister Rockefeller in New York that the state of Colorado is in need of new management. When this strike goes into the winter, and the coal reserves are dried up, and unions in other states are blockading the relief shipments, who do you think voters will hold responsible for making them freeze to death? Make no mistake, Rockefeller's pockets are so deep, he could endorse an orangutan for Governor, and it would win in a landslide!"

Welborn heads for the door, opens it, and looks to Adams one more time. "Think about it." The door closes.

Adams leans back into his chair, loosening his bolo tie. So that was the situation: let the strike continue, endorsing anarchy, or reactivate the Rangers, which amounted to an endorsement of martial law.

A harsh wind is blowing through Capitol Hill in Denver. The colder it gets, the more pressure there will be on his decision. He remembers a line from a school-house history book: "These are the times that try men's souls."

Paine, thinks Adams. It was Thomas Paine who said that. And look what the French did to *him*, when he stood up for his beliefs.

Adams picks up the telephone receiver, and tells the capitol's phone operator to ring the cabinet for an emergency meeting. He'd campaigned on the promise to run the Governor's office like his business, with a tight budget and controlled expenses. When you run a business, Adams thinks to himself, they don't pay you to do nothing.

CHAPTER FIVE

The Prohibition Task Force

Far away, in the heart of the Arkansas River Valley of southern Colorado, a lonely piano tune carries through the streets of Walsenburg. It's coming through the doorjamb of the Walsenburg union hall, the door dangling crosswise from a broken hinge. Men and women outside turn away as they pass the hall, and when they hear the laughter from within the hall, they hurry across the street. The piano is wonky and out-of-tune, and has been ever since the hall was raided last week, and the men now inside threw a Wobbly head-first into the piano keys.

A man is pouring whiskey into a row of shot glasses along the round meeting table. He picks the dribbling glasses up, two in each hand, and passes them around. Square-jawed, with the rugged, wild adventurer look of Charles Lindbergh, Captain Louis Scherf clears his throat.

"A toast, men: the city of Walsenburg sleeps safe again tonight. Raise a glass, grab a gun, we've got the Wobblies on the run!"

No more proof of that was needed than the union hall itself: papers strewn across the floor, the cash box laid bare, and every chair not occupied by one of Scherf's men reduced to matchsticks.

"How many Wobblies in the hospital this time, Captain?" asks a voice from the corner.

Scherf smirks. "Let's just say the local Red rabble won't be marching anywhere soon. Not with Flaming Mamie, at least."

A man straightens himself off the wall, holding a t-bone steak to his face. "Crazy little bitch," says the man. "Put up one hell of a fight."

Scherf pours himself another shot. "Law and order is making a comeback, gentlemen, and just in time for Thanksgiving. This year, I'll bake my turkey over the cinders of Wobbly headquarters."

The phone rings on the wall, Scherf stumbles over. He drains his shot glass in one fiery gulp, and picks up the receiver.

"Prohibition Task Force, Captain Scherf speaking..."

The men in the room, all former Rangers, lean forward, trying to listen in.

At last, Scherf replies with, "We're on our way, sir. Thank you." Scherf hangs up the phone.

"New orders, men! We're headed for some little mine camp called the Columbine!"

The men leap to their feet, but the head rush from the liquor almost forces them back down again. "Which way, Captain?" says a Ranger.

"North," bellows Scherf, "but not as the Prohibition force. The Rangers have been called back into action!"

The men scramble through the room, collecting pistols, bayonets, and shotguns. Scherf walks through the hall, hands behind his back, admiring the hustle of his men. Busting Wobblies for some booze hidden in the floorboards was child's play. Now, the Rangers were back, like Roosevelt's Rough Riders, galloping down the hill, bringing the hammer down on six cartridges of justice.

"All eyes look to the Northern Coal Field for swift resolution," says Scherf. "This strike ends at the Columbine, once and for all!"

The Rangers cheer, and one sits down at the piano bench again, where his fingers find their way through a rendering of the Colorado state song, *Where the Columbines Grow*. They are still singing it as they exit the union hall, and begin their long ride up the Overland Trail...

"The bison has gone from the upland,

The deer from the canyon has fled,

The home of the wolf is deserted,

The antelope mourns for his dead,

The war-whoop re-echoes no longer,

The Indian's only a name,

And the nymphs of the grove in their loneliness rove,

But the Columbine blooms just the same."

CHAPTER SIX

Lead, Kindly Light

Jacques is thinking of his mother as he crouches down into the roadside ditch and removes his shoe. His mind takes him back to a little Frenchtown cottage on Rex Street. His mother is holding him still as she adjusts his denim overalls and hard hat, pointing his carbide lantern straight.

"Now son, don't go out just yet. Eez very important."

Sitting in the ditch, he pulls his sock and bandages off, remembering how impatient he felt with her instructions. His friends would be driving up the street to pick him up soon. His brother's spare overalls feel itchy, he can't wear the others because his brother's blood hasn't completely washed out.

"When ze car pulls up, you no come out."

Jacques remembers nodding, and he pulls a rock from the ground. He smashes it against another rock, it crumbles in his hand.

"When zey honk once, you no come out."

He picks up another rock.

"Zey honk twice, you no come out."

Jacques smashes the rock, it breaks in two with a clean, sharp edge.

"Zey honk sree times, zen you go out, because I want everyone in Frenchtown to know my son eez working this week."

Jacques takes his belt off and sinks his teeth into the leather.

"Lord watch over mon enfant petit today..."

Jacques bites down hard on the belt as he cuts the stone's edge into his blister, and the memories from the house on Rex Street shatter into hot streaks of light. Some men boast about golf games or hunting elk, coal miners boast about how many days they got to work. Nothing made a mother happier than her son working more than any other miner in the neighborhood. That's why Jacques' mother had wanted the friends to honk up a storm.

His mother hadn't said much since he told her about the strike. Dinners were quiet on Rex Street, except when his mother might say something about how Frank would eat here, or used to mine there. She talked about his brother a lot these days. He last saw her just yesterday, after the church service.

After thirty-two miles, Jacques' feet are swollen with blisters, and every few miles, he stops to drain a new one. He tears another strip off his Sunday dress shirt, and wraps it around his foot. The other strips turned solid red long ago.

Jacques looks up, wiping the water from his eyes. He is the first to see the lights coming towards them. He yells out, and the others turn toward the oncoming car. Bell, Eastenes, Ortega, and Jacques are waving, leaping, hollering in each one's native tongue, if they walk one more mile, they are sure to go mad, they need this, just this one kindness, a good Samaritan, oh God, please stop-

The car drives past. Eastenes and the others shield their eyes from the radiant headlights and clouds of dust. They tumble back into a ditch by the road, coughing and groaning. Jacques gets back on his feet, and opens his eyes to find them bathed in starlight. Over a hundred miles from the nearest city, stars burn in the night sky with a dazzling brilliance, and the moon glows bright enough for them to see the highway.

They keep walking.

They have been walking since yesterday afternoon, when they watched the Sheriff's van drive away, shrinking to a black speck on the horizon. They kept walking as their freshly-shined shoes stretched and pulled into scraps of leather, their pressed and starched shirts turned gray with sweat. Dying of exposure in the mid-November air was nothing compared to what their wives were going to do to them, when they saw their husband's best clothes ruined beyond repair. Mary Ortega had spent five weeks washing clothes to pay for Kid Mex's suit, and Jacques' friends sold wine under the table for a month, to a friend-of-a-friend at the Acme Mine. Now Jacques had left that job behind, the job his mother made him wait inside for, until his friends honked their car horn three times. Some son he was.

Eastenes has other matters to consider. Perhaps he could find a tailor in Lafayette who would buy whatever tatters were left of his clothes. That would help put him toward Dorothy's dress. Or maybe the butcher shop on Simpson could let him put the money down for a Thanksgiving ham. He'd joined this stupid strike because of that stupid song, the song that made him fear he'd forget his children's faces. How could he face them now, anyway? Threw away his job in the name of some ideal. Some father.

"What song is that, East?"

Eastenes looks over at Bell. "What song?"

It was Eastenes' bad habit to hum while working, his off-key burblings echoing through the shafts and tunnels without end. Complaints spread from the miners to their wives, until Bertha dragged him to church choir for lessons on Sunday afternoons. He was, and always would be, no real singer, but now he could at least carry a tune, and let his co-workers keep their sanity.

Eastenes tries to remember what, in fact, he had been humming. "It's just something I learned from an old English miner. He told me this story, about a mine explosion in England. One-hundred-fifty dead, instantly.

"A few survivors were trapped in an air pocket, no lanterns. God, it's so dark in those mines, when them lanterns fail. It's like a blackness that's looking into your soul.

"Well, one of those miners, he starts singing this song. Another one joins in, and another. They didn't stop. Singing this song kept them alive in the darkness, until they got rescued. I've been trying to teach it to my little Dorothy. Maybe she could sing it at Christmas mass, or something."

"Teach us."

Eastenes looks over at Ortega, and sees his request is serious. "Nah," says Eastenes, brushing Ortega away. "I'm not like Dorothy. She can sing like her mother."

Bell wipes off his glasses with a strip of his shirt. "It's a long way back to the Columbine camp, East. If we want a chance of making it, I think we're going to need something to sing."

Eastenes looks around, his fellow travelers aren't taking another step without a song on their lips. He sighs, and lets the words come back to him, filling the melody:

"Lead, kindly light, amidst the encircling gloom,

The night is dark, I'm far from home,

Keep thou my feet, I do not ask to see

The distant scene, one step enough for me."

As far as music goes in the coal fields, nothing compares to the Welsh voice choirs. Their sonorous harmonies turned train depots into cathedrals, and the dingy, rat-infested coal tunnels into reverberant concert halls. The miners from Wales worked from childhood in mines that extended far beneath the North Sea, and brought everyone who heard their songs a little closer to the Divine.

Whatever you would call this quartet of marooned picketers, a Latino, a bohunk, a frog, and a soapbox socialist forever without a home, a Welsh choir they are not. They are fortunate that there is no-one around to listen. Still, the words of the old English hymn bring them all nourishment on this lonely highway. Four men, of different lands and languages, who at this point can hardly agree on why they had gone on strike at all, are bound up in this hymn. It unites them all in the singular task they now face: the long road back home.

Bell says they still have another hundred and fifty miles ahead of them. Is that all, thinks Eastenes. We'll make it.

CHAPTER SEVEN

The Girl in Flaming Red

The walk back takes them four days, on account of getting caught outside of Limon and being white-capped again, setting their journey back a full day. They catch a break at Strasburg, the last stop before Denver, and hitch a ride in a vegetable truck.

The four men know something is wrong even before the truck crests the hill at the gate of the Columbine Mine. The sun has set, the door to every cottage is open, men and women tossing their clothing into luggage. Men are gathering across from the offices, fierce arguments surging into frenzies as the disputes come to blows.

Ortega spots Mary and his children trudging with their bags through the mud. He calls her name and breaks into a run.

"Oh Johnny, *idiota!*" cries Mary as they collide in an embrace near the gate. "Where the hell have you been?"

Eastenes feels a tug on his shirt, to find Bertha grabbing him by the collar. She buries her face in his shoulder, sobbing. When Dorothy and his other children pull on his pants, they almost collapse into a pile.

Bell is trying to make sense of just what is going on, when he hears what sounds like an entire schoolhouse stampeding their way. Ortega peeks over Bell's shoulder. "*Madre Mia*, Mrs. Beranek!" whimpers Ortega.

Beranek, rolling pin at her side, is storming towards them with sixteen children and husband in tow.

"Come here, you deadbeats!" Beranek yells, "I'm gonna knock yer blocks off if it's the last thing I do!"

The air is suddenly bursting with the sound of all their children, over two-dozen in total, demanding answers of their own.

"Enough!" yells Beranek. "Mister Bell, the whole world's gone to Perdition, and you're off in some saloon or cat house or I don't know what!"

Bell adjusts his glasses. "Well, Mrs. Beranek, I wouldn't exactly say-"

"And *you!*" Beranek points her rolling pin at Ortega. "My fellow charity tycoon, ha!"

Ortega shakes his head. "No, *señora*, we were white-capped."

Beranek makes a start at him. "Night-cap? I knew it!"

"No!" says Eastenes, "The Sheriff and them deputies kidnapped us. We've been walking for four whole days."

"Hitched a ride from Strasburg this morning" says Ortega.

Jacques sees Spanudakhis and Davis walking past with their suitcases, and grabs them both.

"Nick, what's going on?" asks Jacques.

"Oh, it ain't good, Jay-coo," says the Greek. "The police are raiding our houses every night. The jail is full to the brim!"

Davis points to something in the sky. "Hey! They're coming back again!"

"Who's coming?" is what Eastenes tries to say, but the word "coming" is drowned out by the roar of an engine. His screams are muted as the biplane swoops overhead, loud enough to fill every corner of his brain. When his eyes open, he and everyone else is on the ground. He pulls his fingers from his ears and watches the biplane fly away, so low that Eastenes can make out every last number on the underside. Their children have scattered, Mary, Bertha, and Beranek run off to collect them.

"Not again," says Bell. Planes were a weapon of war against miners in the Long Strike, crushing protest after protest along the southern fields.

"What was that?" asks Ortega.

"The National Guard," says Spanudakhis. "They fly them planes over the camp, all day and all night, until we can't sleep or think."

"And that's just the start of it," says Davis.

Bell looks at Davis. "What else is there, Rookie?"

Davis sighs, and Spanudakhis nudges him. "Tell 'im."

Davis looks back at the Wobbly. "Mister Bell, the militia's back."

Bell says nothing.

"They call themselves the Rangers," says Davis. "Orders from the Governor. Led by some guy named Scarf, Scherf..."

"Wait," says Bell, "*Louis* Scherf?"

"Yeah, that's the one," says Davis.

Bell turns away and pulls off his glasses, cleaning them with what's left of his shirt. When he turns back, every eye is on him. The men hold their wives close, and their children closer.

Bell puts his glasses back on. "The older union men talked about a guy named Pat Hamrock. He led the militia down at the Ludlow Massacre. Hamrock's first lieutenant was Louis Scherf."

Bell watches the hope leave their eyes. Bertha looks up at her husband, and says, "I never liked this. Now they send their dogs after us?"

Eastenes kisses Bertha on the head. "We're lucky we didn't die out on the plains." He looks at Bell. "I have six kids. Maybe you still want to take the risk, but not me, not me, Adam!"

The plane comes over again, and they all dive for cover. Bell watches it head southward, probably refueling. When he looks back, Eastenes is leading his children back to the front gate, headed for Lafayette.

Ludlow, thinks Bell, it's Ludlow all over again. In his mind, the White City burns.

"Mister Bell?"

Bell looks down at Davis.

"We are going to call a vote, on whether to continue the strike or not."

Bell looks at his friends, and the teeming tableau of miners scrambling beneath the tipple. Now he understands the miner's sensation of it crashing down on you.

"We were close," says Bell. "I could feel it." Bell straightens his frayed Sunday jacket and scrapes some dried mud off. "It's been an honor to stand alongside you."

Just then, a car horn blares down on the county line road. "Is it the cops again?" asks Jacques.

Bell adjusts his glasses, his eyes tracing the road down to the highway. The car is an Oakland two-cylinder, like what the Wobblies drive down south. He could see the picketers sitting up from the grass to follow the car up the hill.

It can't be, thinks Bell. She was arrested...

A great throng of cheering bodies is following the car now, a tidal wave through the open gate. The car door opens, and Bell can't even see her with all the people in the way. Women rush from cottage to cottage, spreading the word, followed by a stream of families from every front door.

A group of miners run to the trash heap behind the office, grabbing broken mine cart sidings, wood pallets, and used powder boxes.

In two minutes, a makeshift stage is hammered together from the debris, and in the darkening twilight, the miners pull out their carbide lamps, each light focused on the forum.

The stage wobbles and bends, even under the girl's slight weight, and the crowd is cheering so hard she stays silent for a full minute. Six weeks ago, the Wobblies had put out a call for every foot-loose rebel to come to Colorado and fight the good fight. She had been arrested, all right, in the mighty march up Delagua Canyon, and yet, by escape or early release, here she is.

Flaming Mamie looks out on the crowd, her red dress burning like the furnace of Nebuchadnezzar amidst the gray coal ash and dead grass of the hillside. November had brought with it that bitter wind that cuts through a miner's layers of wool and denim, and here is Mamie in that red dress.

The crowd quiets down at last, and Flaming Mamie speaks.

"Every last one of you came from somewhere else. Our parents, from Croatia." She points to Ortega. "You, your people, Mexico.

Greece. France. Bohemia. But I am not Croatian. You are not Mexican, or a frog, or a Greek, or a bohunk."

Mamie unfurls the long length of cloth in her hands. A familiar sight: forty-eight stars, thirteen stripes, red, white, and blue.

"I'm an American!"

The crowd cheers, and she takes long steps along the creaking stage, letting her American flag shine bright in the glow of the carbide lanterns.

"In a week, it will be Thanksgiving. All of us came here to America in search of a better life, just like them Pilgrims on the first Thanksgiving. And yet when we try to speak free, they call us criminals. When we ask to be paid enough to live, they call us socialists!"

She hocks a wad of spit into the dirt, as sure as any tobacco marksman. "I'm not attacking America. I'm defending what it means to be an American!

"We dig the coal that burns in every home, that powers every street light, that runs every train, and for our hard work, they fly their warbirds overhead to drive us crazy!"

"It's not right!" cries Beranek.

"To beat hell!" shouts Bertha.

"To beat hell!" shouts little Dorothy, and Bertha cups her hand around her daughter's mouth as the crowd laughs.

Mamie waves a finger across the crowd, eyes making contact with each one in the multitude. "When you struck in 1893, nothing changed. When you took to the streets in 1903, nothing changed. When they slaughtered your wives and daughters at Ludlow, and shot poor Louis Tikas in the back, nothing changed. They still cheat you at the weigh machine. Pay you so little you have to hunt rabbits in the fields to eat. Pay you with scrip, and tell you that you can't form no union, to speak as one. When they blew the three whistles at the Vulcan, and the Hastings, you asked the mines be made safe, but nothing's changed.

"They have you down for the count, they think they took the heart out of ya. And maybe they did. If you ask me, you give up this time, you give it up for good.

"But if you get back on your feet, and stand together, no matter how much it hurts, no matter what names they call you, you still stand a chance. People, for generations to come, will remember how you chose to stand for something good and right. They'll remember you fought to have a voice, you fought to be free, you fought to give your children a better tomorrow.

"So now, you wives and miners, I'm telling you to get back up again, and every time they knock us down, and call us dirty foreigners, to go back where we came from, I want you to get right back up and tell them all, 'I'm an American, and I'm not going anywhere!'"

The roar of the crowd that night was louder than any airplane that could have flown overhead. Along the barbed wire fence, and on the high tipple, the guards and Rangers watch the miners celebrate in the chill autumn air.

That night, the Union Hall in Lafayette rings with the songs of the old country. These men and women come from nations that had waged war across Europe and Central America for centuries, but here, tonight, their joy was shared joy, their struggle, shared struggle. Little Dorothy, and Lupie, Ortega's oldest daughter, watch their parents dance on the worn-down hardwood. Eastenes and Bertha look at each other, more in love now than they could have ever believed possible. How could that not be the case, when they had met at a dance just like this, and after one date had decided to marry? They had barely known each other then, but now life had taught them what the other was made of, and it was beautiful.

The miner's families clear room for Ortega, and he wows the crowd with that lightning footwork that won the champion's belt. When he was in his prime, Ortega, a mere featherweight, had been the headliner, and Jack Dempsey, the legendary Manassa Mauler, why, *he'd* been the undercard fight! And yet, he was glad to have it behind him. Coal mining was a technical trade, and with his body in top shape, and a good head on his shoulders, he could keep at it for some time. A boxer, though, washed-up, punch-drunk, with no other skills to sell, well, a man like that can't take care of his *esposa, o sus hijos*.

Ortega stops, resting his hands on his knees to cough. He looks up and sees Beranek, and her husband Joe, teaching their children the dances of their own childhoods. They just about take up half the Union Hall. After Mamie's speech, Beranek was the one who had called the vote to continue the strike, before anyone else had a chance. Before the resounding "Yes" had left the lips of every miner there, she had begun marching off toward the line of cars at the bottom of the hill, for a ride to the Simpson Mine. She'd heard they had stashed a few supplies, and wanted to negotiate. Not a moment to lose. Ortega wonders what might have happened if this strange force of nature hadn't been standing there at the gate when his cage came up from the shaft. Maybe they'd still be in this hall, or maybe he'd be back down in those tunnels, on a night shift, hunched over a four-foot seam.

The young Jerry Davis has no woman in his life, but a meeting with Flaming Mamie more than makes up for that. At the back of the dance hall, she hands him an American flag. She tells Davis that the hope for freedom grows when that flag waves in the sky. That flag has seen America through its darkest nights, and if they fly that flag proudly, freedom might live another day.

Davis carries the flag in his arms on the ride home to Frederick, east of the Columbine, and hangs it on the wall by his bed. He wonders if, being a dangerous, exotic labor advocate and all, Mamie's been to every state with a star on that flag. She's probably been to all sorts of far-off places, like Moscow, Caracas, and Minnesota.

Davis falls asleep, the twangs of the Union Hall music still clamoring in his ears.

INTERLUDE

or, The Bigger Bloodsucker

Sean and Gerry follow Glava through the rows of headstones, watching the spirits of the cemetery reset the stage during intermission. Gerry notices Glava sipping from a glass dripping with bright, viscous red.

"What's that?" asks Gerry. "Virgin's blood?"

Glava finishes off the glass. "Clamato juice. High in sodium, but I'm already dead, so, you know, not a problem. What do you think of this journey so far, children? Is the Not-So-Long-Ago as boring as you once imagined?"

"No," says Sean with a sigh.

"How about you, Gerry?" says Glava. "Something on your mind?"

"My dad told me about these unions," says Gerry. "He told me most of them were really corrupt."

"Compared to who?" says Sean. "Who's paying people with fake money, beating them up? The mines, not the unions."

Gerry shrugs. "My dad and uncle used to work for a big snack food company back east. He said the union wouldn't let you tie your own shoelaces if it wasn't in your job description. My dad got so sick of it we moved out here."

Sean can't believe it. "So I guess stuff like eight-hour work days, child labor laws, sick leave, companies just did that out of the goodness of their hearts, huh?"

"At least they could work," says Gerry, looking at the spirit's Columbine stage. "At least they had jobs!"

"Now you're sounding like those Rangers!" says Sean.

Gerry rolls his eyes and turns to Glava. "Maybe you can tell us, being a vampire. Who was the bigger bloodsucker, the mines, or the unions?"

Glava shakes his tousled mane. "I speak for the spirits of this cemetery, who lived in a world far different from your own. It is up to you, children, to decide if their story is little more than the curiosities of a tired past, or lessons that will carry across time..."

CHAPTER EIGHT

They Won't Even Know It

John Eastenes stands just outside of the cage door on the surface of the Columbine, and pushes in the plunger on the blasting machine. He feels the ground convulse beneath his feet as the dynamite blasts open a coal seam, hundreds of feet below them. He looks over at Ortega, who nods, and Eastenes pulls the blasting machine's plunger back up, removing the wires from the nodes on the front. Ortega, standing with Rudy the mule, pulls the straps tight on the mule's supply sack.

The blasting machine sends an electric current down to a set of blasting caps, small bombs that plug holes in the coal room walls, stuffed with dynamite. They'll load the dislodged coal into a cart, and bring it up to the surface. It was simple enough, but the trick was doing it and living to tell the tale.

Eastenes and Ortega hear the sharp hiss of the steam hoists fade away with every yard the cage descends into the earth. The mule couldn't care less. Eastenes thinks he hears a dog bark back on the surface. Their eyes moisten as the air becomes thick with coal dust, Eastenes hacks into his shoulder. The cage slams to a halt, and the door opens onto thick clouds of black.

The dynamite explosion knocked the coal out of the walls, and kicked up hundreds of pounds of raw dust. Eastenes wheezes, shuts his eyes. They can't see the smoke in the pitch black, but they can feel it burrowing into their lungs, into every pore. They are blind, led only by the tail of the mule. Eastenes tries to remember the words to the old hymn, the one that got them through that walk across the plains, but the words fly away before he can catch them. All he can think of is how much coal must be in his lungs, after all these years. Hell, he started working down here when he was only ten years old.

They feel the pressure change, and know the tunnel has opened up into the coal room. Eastenes trips over a lump of coal, the ground is piled high with them. Groping in the dark, they pat each other on the back. They'll make good money off this seam. Visions of glistening-white turkey meat just about washes the coal dust from their mouths, and it's at that very moment the failed charge goes off in their faces.

The blast throws Eastenes into a corner of the room, his head slams against the wall, ears ringing, face streaming blood. One of the blasting caps must have failed to explode on time, and now they walked right into it. Ortega was closest to the blast, dead for sure, and he hears the last few drops of life drain from the mule into a warm pool on the rock floor. Eastenes' mind is nothing but an operating manual now: crawl back to the cage, ring the alarm...

But it's too late. Eastenes can see light in the pitch-black room, the last cinders of the blasting cap kissing a few molecules of coal dust. The entire tunnel is full of coal dust, giving off "fire-damph," methane. Eastenes may as well be standing in a bathtub of gasoline.

The air comes alive in beautiful, twisting vortices of red and yellow, the flames are voracious, sucking the oxygen from his lungs before he can scream. The tongues of fire surge up before him, igniting the clothes on his back, he finds his last cheekful of air, screaming out into the night-

And Eastenes sees it *is* night, back in his bed in Lafayette.

Eastenes blinks away the sweat pouring down his face, choked up on the pain of his heart pounding inside his chest. He unclenches his hands, letting go of a now-crumpled Sears-Roebuck catalog, the one he fell asleep reading. Bertha lies next to him, still sound asleep in spite of his nightmare. Bertha has become the talk of the town for her soups, driving around the coal field, serving it at relief lines. Even in this time of need, people have been willing to buy her recipe, and from that they have earned enough money to buy Dorothy's dress.

He is thankful to have met the strange companions he now called friends: Bell, Ortega, Jacques, Spanudakhis. If he's being honest with himself, he isn't sure if he'd let any of their children marry his, and he's pretty sure they feel the same way. Such is life in an immigrant town. What he does know for sure, though, is that they'd had his back through this whole ordeal. Whatever might come between them, the strike held them together. They all believed in those things Flaming Mamie had talked about.

Thanksgiving is five days away, come next morning. Eastenes was thankful his family had come here from Bohemia, and not stayed behind. Europe was nothing but war, famine, and plague. To be sure, they had that here, too, but they also had a chance to own land, to build a house, a chance at a future. You were sure to find none of that back in Bohemia. In America, you could dream, and it was worth fighting to make that dream come true.

Outside the window, a dog barks, followed by the screech of a cat, and Lafayette descends into darkness.

* * * *

At that very moment, out at the Columbine Mine, Captain Louis Scherf is watching a large box truck begin climbing the hill. A new shipment, he's told, and he looks over at the mine tipple as the floodlight passes over it, illuminating the skeletal figures shuffling into the cage, courtesy of the last shipment.

When Scherf looks back toward the truck, he sees the streetlights of Lafayette have disappeared in the distance, leaving a black hole in the landscape.

"Look at that, men" says Scherf to his Rangers. "The power outages have begun. I bet they ran out of coal at the power plant, the reserves are dry. That's what these Wobbly scoundrels want for us, a world of darkness. Well, not on my watch. Tomorrow is the beginning of the end for the Wobblies, and they won't even know it."

* * * *

Back in Lafayette, the cats and dogs seem to have ended their war for the night, and in the few minutes of darkness before the power comes back on, Eastenes feels his heart return to a normal beat, and falls asleep.

The next morning, a few blocks from Eastenes' house, an inspector from Western Light & Electric leans his ladder against a utility pole. He reaches up between the high-voltage lines, and his rubber gloves grab hold of the cause of last night's power outage. He pulls it free, and drops the charred remains of a cat into the rubbish bin.

CHAPTER NINE

Coffee and Donuts

The morning after the power outage, the picketers make their daily march to the Columbine Mine. A long line of picketers has formed, waiting to join the others at the front gate. Jerry Davis paces the line up and down. A long stick hangs from Davis' shoulders, from which hang a dozen dead rabbits.

"Rabbits, rabbits here! Get yer rabbits, fresh from the hills!"

Davis sells half his quarry in under a minute, making a whole seventy-five cents. The strikers have been eating pinto beans, and nothing but, for a solid month now. Pinto beans, three meals a day, until they have to will themselves into thinking they taste like strawberries. In that frame of mind, the dry meat of a jackrabbit was like an ice cream sundae.

Davis steps to the front of the line, where Spanudakhis is patting a striker down.

"Whaddaya know?" says Davis, "It's the Greek! It looks like you're the foreman now, deciding who gets in."

The Greek replies, "Yeah, well the foreman says open your coat, Rookie."

"What are you talking about?" says Davis.

"You know what I'm talking about" says Spanudakhis. Davis sighs, and holds his arms up. Spanudakhis pats him down. He pulls a long billy club out of the young man's coat.

Spanudakhis frowns. "You know the rules, Rookie."

Davis protests, "Aw, come on, Nick!"

"No," says the Greek, "No weapons in the picket line, ever."

"How do you think I got those rabbits?" asks Davis. "With my foul mouth? Look, I forgot, okay?"

"Not okay," says the Greek. "If them Rangers think we're bringing weapons in, they won't need no reason to come after us. Old Adam Bell, he says we have to be the better men. Or boys, in your case."

Davis smiles, shakes a fist. "You're asking for it now, you dumb Greek!" He hands a couple rabbits to Spanudakhis, and walks over to the picketers at the front gate. "Rabbits! Rabbits fresh from the hills!"

Eastenes walks over to Spanudakhis, who hands Eastenes the club and a rabbit. "Put the club on the truck back to Frederick, the Rookie can pick it up there."

Eastenes tosses the club into a nearby truck bed, and looks at their rabbits, which are almost as thin as they are.

"Rabbits for three days now, Nick," says Eastenes. "Think we're going to get sick of 'em?"

The Greek holds his rabbit up, looking into its dead eyes. "I think we're going to find out, one way or another."

Over in the crowd of picketers, Beranek stands in a circle with the other women. The wives, and a few daughters, have been front and center at these pickets, maybe even more than the miners. When a miner is underpaid for his work, and driven to spend it all at a speakeasy, it was as much an injustice on his wife and children as it was on the miner. In the Long Strike, it was old Mother Jones who led the women of Trinidad against a charge of cavalry militiamen. It was Mary Miller, mother and banker in equal parts, who lent money to miners in their time of need. It was wives and little ones who paid the mortal price at Ludlow, as fires swept over the tent colony.

The women at the picket have discussed the usual daily necessities of blankets, and the next charity organization to petition with letters. Their conversation now turns to that strange and indispensable alchemy known to women, a sorcery by which armies are sustained, men fall in love, and the great cities of the world earn their reputations. In America, they call it "cooking," and in a strike, when food is hard to come by, cooking is everything.

Beranek finishes jotting a list in her journal. "So, that's nine more ways to cook pinto beans."

Mary Ortega laughs. "If my kids have pinto bean one more night, they will turn into a pinto."

"I'll tell you what," says Beranek. "One more good idea before we leave. Two extra bags of pinto to the best one!"

Bertha's hand shoots up. "Oh! How about a little Polish sausage?"

"We're running low on meat," says Beranek, "unless it's jackrabbit."

"We found a little bit in the cellar last night," says Bertha.

"Si," says Mary, "and what if I added a little bit of chili pepper, and tomato? That's a real meal right there!"

Beranek rubs her chin. "Polish chili? Heck, at this point, I'll try anything you put in front of me." She tosses one bag of raw pinto each to Bertha and Mary. "Have it ready by tomorrow morning!"

Ortega catches his wife with a little kiss on the cheek as he passes by with a large ledger book. "Let's see," he says, "that's five old coats for the Simpson Mine camp, some kerosene from the Monarch in Louisville, *gracias, Señor* Jacques..."

"Pas de quoi, Monsieur Ortega!" says Jacques.

Ortega looks around and shouts, "Now, *quien necesita?"*

Eastenes raises a hand from the weapons-check line. "Bertha's running a little low on kerosene."

"How much can she live with?" asks Ortega.

"Maybe a half-quart?" says Eastenes.

Ortega gestures off toward Lafayette. "Meet Beranek at her house."

Davis calls from the other side of the picket line, "I heard Vidovitch up in Erie has more rabbits!"

Ortega yells back, "Tell him to bring a few to the Union Hall on Simpson Street!" Already, Union Hall had the appearance of being constructed entirely from rabbit pelts, a great furry box with feet protruding at all angles, and a thousand black, glassy eyes.

Mary comes over to her husband. "Did I hear there were some old coats?"

"A few," says Ortega. "Do we need more?"

"There's been some, what is it, *la tos ferina*, in the camp. I'm worried that our littlest one has it."

"Tos ferina," says Eastenes, "You mean whooping cough?"

"Yes, that's it," says Mary. In cramped company housing, disease spread like a flash flood crashing down Boulder Canyon. Houses were close together, and the long distance to the nearest town kept the healthy packed in with the sick.

"Hey Kid Mex," says Eastenes. "I still have my blanket Beranek got me, and what's left of my suit from when we got white-capped. You can have them."

Ortega smiles. *"Gracias, amigo."*

The old boxer sees Bell running up the hill to the picketers, panting.

"Everyone, listen up!" yells Bell.

"Escúchalo!" yells Ortega. The crowd falls silent.

Bell speaks. "I just got a telegram from Walsenburg. This is it, folks!"

Murmurs in the crowd. "What's it?" asks Davis.

Bell is downright elated. "Every coal mine in Colorado has shut down, except for this one, right here!"

The crowd explodes into cheers.

"Brothers and sisters!" shouts Bell, "Brothers and sisters! I've picketed across this nation, I've been beaten up and left on the edge of town more times than I care to recall, but this, this, my friends, is the closest we've ever come. This time, they're going to listen to us." The crowd erupts once again, Bell adds, "I promise you that."

As the applause fades, Bell hears one more pair of hands clapping behind him, and a voice adding, "Bravo, hear, hear!"

They turn to see Captain Scherf, dressed head-to-toe in full Ranger uniform. The rough-and-tumble cowboy getup of the Prohibition Task Force has been replaced by polished brass stars, and boots that shine like mirrors. The other Rangers form a phalanx behind Scherf, and from out of the office, why, here comes Sheriff Robinson, fixing his hat and pulling his trousers straight.

Scherf extends a hand to Bell.

"I'm Captain Louis Scherf. Don't mind me and my men, we're just here to keep the peace."

Bell regards the Captain, and asks, "And how do you plan on keeping the peace, Captain Scherf?"

Scherf grins. "Why, the best way I know how: coffee, and donuts!"

Bell watches the Rangers carry a long table from the Foreman's office to the mine gate, topped with with a platter of donuts and a cauldron-like coffee pot. A crowd of picketers encircles Scherf and his table of treats. He cups his hands around his mouth, yelling, "Coffee! Coffee and donuts, courtesy of your new president!"

"New president?" asks Eastenes.

Scherf pours some coffee into a ceramic mug, and hands it to a picketer. "The Rocky Mountain Fuel Company is under new management. A certain Miss Josephine Roche has inherited the Columbine Mine from her father. She has instructed us to make clear we mean no harm, and offer food and drink, so long as you keep to your side of the gate."

Scherf looks around at the wary faces, eyeing the donuts. "What, you think it's poisoned?" snaps Scherf, and he stuffs a donut into his mouth. *"Shee, ish delishish!"*

The strikers come forward, and the high donut pyramid begins to shrink. Everything about Scherf rubs Ortega wrong. He's wondered about these Rangers whom Bell speaks of in strained whispers, who so far have spent most of their time at the Columbine talking in the Foreman's office. He doesn't like Scherf's smiles game. Down in the boxing rings of Pueblo, it was always the boxer who talked about a "good, clean fight" that seemed itching to piss on your grave.

Ortega hears the puff of a diesel engine, and sees a truck making its way up the hill. Scherf's head perks up. "Ah, still more new shipments for us!"

The truck pulls into the gate, and the driver steps out to open the back door. For the first time in thirteen years, Ortega feels physically sick. The men shambling out of the rear of the truck share Ortega's brown skin, but their eyes are lifeless, their cheeks hollowed from hunger, clothing in rags.

Scherf pats Ortega on the shoulder. "Someone has to mine the coal, buddy. These fine gentlemen from..." Scherf looks down at some papers, "*Coo-ah-hoo-ee-la-day-Zara-goza*, from grand old *Mee-hee-ko*, were more than happy to take the jobs you and your 'comrades' just threw away."

Ortega walks up to one of the imported scabs, a man so tired his head bobs up and down, eyelids fluttering.

"*Como te llamas?*" Ortega asks him. *"Habla Ingles? Sabes dónde estás?"*

Ortega understands the man's words, words the man has learned to say as a means of survival: "I need a pick and an auger, show me to the store. I need a pick and an auger, show me to the store, I need a-"

The man grunts as a Ranger shoves him forward with the butt of his shotgun. Ortega lets the man go, and turns back to Scherf.

"These men don't even speak English!" says Ortega. "You truck them up here like cattle to work under the barrel of a gun!" Ortega points to the machine gun now mounted atop the mine tipple.

Scherf laughs. "That's for their own protection, in case you try interfering with proper business."

"No," seethes Ortega, "It's to keep them your slaves, since *we* refused to be slaves any longer!"

Bell smiles. He knows most of the strikers don't care about politics, or the socialist utopia the Wobblies pledged to realize. Watching Ortega, though, he thinks to himself, "And that is how a Wobbly is born: standing against the injustice done to your fellow worker."

Scherf's eyes narrow on Ortega, and for a moment the boxer thinks the Ranger Captain will lose his cool. "Easy there, son, this is the Rangers. Our forebears kept the Confederacy out of Colorado when they hungered for our gold mines. Shoot, we probably won the whole war on account of that."

Ortega nods. "*Si*, and then Colonel Chivington took his men down to Sand Creek and butchered the Indians."

"A historian, huh?" exclaims Scherf. "I don't think I got your name."

"Careful, Captain," says another Ranger. "That's Johnny Kid Mex. I saw him box down south, he's laid a few guys flat in the ring."

Scherf tilts his head back, grinning. "I see. The Wobblies got a celebrity endorsement. I like it!"

"I'm no celebrity, Captain," says Ortega.

"No," says Eastenes, "Kid Mex is my friend. Just a man like me, trying to make things better for his family."

"Like all of us," says Ortega.

Scherf keeps on smiling, and heads back for the office, the Rangers following him. "All the same, get the coffee while it's hot."

* * * *

Meanwhile, at the State Capitol in Denver, Governor Adams drops the latest issue of the *Boulder Daily Camera* on his desk. Lucius C. Paddock has been using his newspaper to rail on the strike all week, and today is no exception. Adams scans the editorial section, and finds Paddock has a message for him:

"Machine guns are the best answer to picketers," writes Paddock. *"When posted at the Columbine, willing workers go to work while picketers slink back. Machine guns manned by willing shooters are wanted at other Colorado mines, Governor Adams."*

Adams slaps the paper. "Just what I need! Paddock throwing more chum into the water, starting a feeding frenzy!"

He collapses into his chair. He now understands why every US President seems to undergo premature aging. He was merely the Governor, but in his years in politics, he'd had to put down the Ku Klux Klan, oversee construction on the Moffat, the longest train tunnel in the world, and commission a new state college in his hometown, which they had been so generous to name after him. Now, the state faces a crisis that made all others pale in comparison. He rubs his temples, longing for the days when his hardest choice was which cowboy hat to wear.

* * * *

Back at the Columbine Mine, Sheriff Robinson peers out through the shutters of the Foreman's office, watching the picketers finish off the last of the coffee and donuts. Scherf sits with his feet on a card table, playing poker with his men, eyeing a pair of one-eyed jacks in his hand.

Scherf isn't sure who's ordering these strike-breakers in from Mexico, who do indeed appear to have been Shanghaied, or bought wholesale from a chain-gang labor camp. It might be the Columbine's competitor CF&I, or the Governor's office, or a rogue company board member, but he's not paid enough to know those things.

Even so, he can appreciate the thought process. If the coal companies could keep a single mine open (not counting his old boss Hamrock's failed attempt with the prisoners at Cañon City), then they could still say the strike was a failure. The Wobblies couldn't close them all.

Furthermore, the Columbine held a strategic position. The strike had taken CF&I by surprise down south, and in the north, mines had real towns nearby to sustain a strike. The Columbine, with its fenced-in housing, cut off from the rest of the world by several miles, could keep picketers out, and strike-breakers locked in (not that those poor Mexicans had a prayer if they tried running). Try as they might, a scab who was brought to the Columbine was there to stay.

Sheriff Robinson steps away from the window. "Captain Scherf, may I have a word?"

"It's a free country," says Scherf.

Robinson pulls up his trousers again. "I don't know about you, but Weld County didn't elect me Sheriff to hand out coffee and donuts. We should be out there arresting those people!"

"Yeah, what's the idea?" says Scherf's poker partner. "Is this the Salvation Army or what?"

"At ease, men" says Scherf. He drops two cards from his hand, adds two more. The pair of one-eyed jacks have become a three-of-a-kind. "You don't know it yet, but we are on the eve of our victory."

"Coffee is victory?" asks Robinson.

"Indeed it is, Sheriff." Scherf takes his winnings after his Ranger hold-out folds. "The best way to win a battle, men, is to make the enemy *think* they've won. I've known women like Josephine Roche. Lily-livered progressives. Every mine owner's daughter is like that, swear to God. If she wants her former employees to have their coffee, let them. They think the Rocky Mountain Fuel Company is on the verge of caving in to them, and when they think victory is in sight, they'll let their guard down. At that moment, we spring our trap."

Robinson lets out a weak laugh. "Uh, and what trap is that, Captain?"

Five minutes later, Scherf, the Rangers, and a white-faced Robinson exit the office. Scherf sees a little girl eating the last donut.

"Got your fill yet?" asks Scherf.

"Thank you, sir!" says Dorothy.

"You can thank the new mine owner," says Scherf, "she's a kindhearted woman." Scherf turns back to his men, muttering, "We'll see where that gets her in the coal business."

Dorothy looks down, blushes, and pulls another donut out of her dress pocket. "May I take this one home to my brothers?"

Scherf chuckles, and leans down to Dorothy's height. "I don't see why not." He picks his Ranger hat off his head and drops it on Dorothy's.

Scherf straightens up, and watches Dorothy skip away. His attention turns back to Ortega.

"So, Johnny Kid Mex. You know, I used to do some boxing, back in Officer's Training. Maybe we can go a few rounds some time, a friendly exhibition match."

Ortega finishes his coffee, setting the mug back on the table. "A pleasure meeting you, Captain." Ortega leaves.

Bell is observing the exchange when he feels a hand sink into his shoulder. He grimaces, and spins around to see a pale, sweating Sheriff Robinson.

"You got me, Sheriff." Bell raises his hands up. "Hook me, and book me."

"No, not that!" says Robinson. "Listen to me: stay out of here for a while."

Bell suppresses a laugh. "Sheriff, to quote a most beautiful and smart young lady, 'I'm an American, and I'm not going anywhere.'"

The surrounding picketers applaud, and Robinson's eyes dart over to Scherf, who isn't paying attention, or at least doesn't appear to be. He wipes beads of hot sweat from his forehead.

"You don't understand," he says, cocking his head. *"It's not your day, see?* Don't come around here again. I'll be forced to arrest you! This time, I'll drop you off in North Dakota!"

Bell puts his arm around Robinson, and moves him toward the crowd. "Sheriff, we were just planning a parade up north to Erie. I think you should be our guest of honor."

The crowd approves, and pushes Robinson toward the motorcade, bedecking him with garlands and union accessories. The motorcade drives off toward Erie, ignoring the Sheriff's repeated demands to stay away from the Columbine.

CHAPTER TEN

Union Hall

The kerosene lamp burns low in the Union Hall of Lafayette, casting long shadows across the wooden floor. Ortega, Beranek, and Bell stand around a stack of papers, deciding who will lead the next day's chants, who'll check the crowd for weapons, who will be cooking, who will...

Bell stretches his arms out and yawns. The wall clock's pendulum swings back and forth, reading half-past midnight. November 21st now. Bell resolves to work another hour.

"Who's making the soup tomorrow?" asks Bell.

Beranek finishes the last of her donation requests to local organizations: Odd Fellows, Order of the Eastern Star, Pythian Sisters, Rebekahs, Macabees, and the Lignite Lodge of the Knights of Pythias. "Bertha has it in the pot right now."

"Right," says Bell, "the Polish chili." They're too tired to laugh.

"I need to head back to the camp," says Ortega. "Mary is looking after the little ones, my youngest has *la tos ferina*, the whooping cough."

Beranek thanked God every day that she hadn't lost one of hers to whooping cough. It was a dark, hollow cough that kept children in bed for weeks. She remembers the hours spent at the bedside, holding damp cloth to a child's forehead. How many mothers did she know, who could say they had seen all of their children make it through childhood? She needed no holiday to be thankful for that.

The three of them bolt up as they hear a loud knock at the door. Beranek is closest, and she heaves her tired body up from the table to open the door. Jerry Davis is standing under the cold electric streetlight, panting hard.

"Mrs. Beranek," Davis wheezes out.

Bell looks over Beranek's shoulder. "Whaddaya know, Rookie? I heard you were hunting up some more rabbits tonight."

Davis regains his breath. "I was hunting up in the hills, and passed by the Columbine. The gates… the gates were locked."

Beranek looks at Bell and Ortega, back at Davis. "You… you mean the gates were *closed*."

Davis shakes his head. "No, locked up, with big, heavy chains. When I came closer, they turned the floodlight my way, and them Rangers pointed their guns at me. I ran back here."

Bell steps away from the door, and Beranek can see his eyes darting here and there, deep in thought. Bell turns back to Davis. "Run down to the company store, Jerry. Tell me if it's locked up. Not closed, locked up, understand?"

"I know the one," says Davis, and he runs off down the street.

Bell leaves the threshold, pacing the Union Hall. In his head, he calculates that it will take Davis a good minute to run down to Iowa Avenue, a little longer to come back, with the hill. "No, they wouldn't do that," he mumbles to himself. "But the Sheriff, he said 'It's not your day.'"

Ortega crosses the room to face Bell. In the soft shadows of the kerosene light, Ortega's face is painted in dark lines. The orange flame catches the first whispers of something desperate in his eyes.

"Adam, my family is inside that camp," says Ortega. "They're in that camp with them Rangers, and their guns."

Bell looks away from Ortega. "Johnny, they're just trying to provoke us."

"Then they're doing a damn good job!"

They hear footsteps behind them, and see Davis back at the still-open door. "Well?" snaps Ortega.

"There's a padlock on the door," says Davis, "big as my fist. All the windows are barred, too."

Ortega steps away from Bell, staring out past Davis with blank eyes into a black night, and whispers, "They're trapped. They've caged my family..."

Ortega bolts for the door, and Davis spreads his limbs across the doorjamb to block the way. The boxer seizes Davis' shirt in his fist to hurl him aside, but Beranek and Bell pull him back in, pleading with him to stop. It takes the strength of all three to bring Ortega down into a chair.

"Get off me!" Ortega screams. "I'll rip those *pendejos* limb from limb!"

Bell grabs Ortega's shoulders. "That's just what they want us to do! Back in the Long Strike, the strikers used guns and arson to fight the mine companies. All that did was give the companies an excuse. When the company thugs sent a miner to the morgue, sometimes the miners returned the favor. When the guards set fire to Ludlow, they called it self-defense. That's why we can't use violence, we can't make it easy for them."

Ortega sits in the chair, holding his head in his hands. Bell straightens up, speaking to Beranek and Davis. "We march for the Columbine before dawn. They have no legal basis to lock us out. Johnny, I'm sure you want to split the head of every Ranger up there, and a good deal of me wants to join you, but it's why I'm going to ask you to stay here with Beranek."

"And why am I staying here?" she asks.

"I don't want any women or children there," says Bell. "Just a sensible precaution."

Beranek steps forward, eyes narrowing. "Mister Bell, do you think my womanhood makes me unfit for the front lines? I've brought sixteen children into this world, Adam. It will take more than a few company thugs to stop me."

Bell sighs, and nods to her. He looks back at Ortega, slumped in the chair, "Go, then," he says. "Bring back my family. I won't make it easy for them." Ortega looks up, "But you better promise me it'll be the last easy day they have."

Bell doesn't respond, no point in lying, and points to Beranek.

"Wake everyone up, tell them what happened. I'll make sure the cars are ready."

Bell leaves with Davis, and Beranek pulls the telephone receiver off its cradle. "Operator," she says, "get me the Spanudakhis house on Cleveland Street."

In his fighting days, John Ortega had taken on the best boxers in the Rockies, but tonight, he feels truly helpless. The thought of his wife and children trapped in that coal camp, the youngest sick with whooping cough, will stay with him for the rest of his life. The story of the miners is almost over. The first rays of sunlight will soon rise over the roofs of the Columbine.

CHAPTER ELEVEN

Dawn at the Columbine

Scherf works a wad of tobacco in his teeth, his eyes fixed beyond the padlocked gate of the mine camp, crisscrossed with chains and barbed wire. The sky is still deep blue in the pre-dawn. Scherf's men are strapped with rifles, shotguns, bayonets and pistols. The fresh-pressed uniforms and mirror-shine boots are gone, back to the utilitarian clothing of their Prohibition days. Scherf had made it clear to his men that you didn't wear your best clothing when taking out the trash. The uniform deserves better.

A Ranger has been sent up to the roof of the mine tipple to man the machine gun, its long barrel tracing an arc across the dark horizon of the Rockies.

The men are shivering in the cold, rigid thumbs braced against their safety catches and trigger-guards.

"Steady, men," says Scherf. "Today, I'm going to teach you how to put down an insurrection. There's one man in charge of this whole Wobbly snake-pit, and when I find him, I'm putting him on the express train to Purgatory. These simple miner types are always looking for a top dog to lead them, like the Philistines to Goliath. Cut the head off..." Scherf turns to the Rangers, and drags a thumb across his throat, "... The body dies."

The Ranger's hoots of approval are cut short by a quick whistle from the guard on the tipple. Scherf looks up, and follows the guard's pointing finger past the gate.

The picketers crest the hilltop, five hundred men and women approaching the perimeter fence. American flags float like islands above the sea of faces, and Scherf can hear the low chants of 'Solidarity' emanating from the crowd. They arrive at the gate, and Beranek steps forward.

"Sir, let us in," she says. "We just want to see our friends and families."

Scherf grits his teeth, firing a wad of tobacco juice onto the ground. He rests one hand on his service pistol and yells out to the crowd.

"Who is your leader?"

Bell is about to announce himself, and Scherf's eyes widen in anticipation, but a voice calls out from Bell's right.

"We're all leaders!" shouts Davis.

"We're all leaders!" shouts Spanudakhis.

"We're all leaders!" shout Jacques and Eastenes. The cry spreads in waves across the crowd.

Scherf looks back at the Rangers, uneasy, and yells back over the picketers. "The mine's closed today. In the name of the law, back away and go home."

"Captain Scherf, is it?"

Scherf looks back down at the old man approaching the fence. "That's the name," says Scherf. He takes a step toward the gate, until Scherf and Bell are kept apart only by the barbed wire.

Bell takes out his law book. "Captain Scherf, this mining camp has a United States Post Office. Under Title IV, Chapter 17, Section 481 of the US Postal Laws, we have a legal right to access our mail."

Scherf grimaces. "You can get your mail tomorrow."

Bell flips a page without looking up at Scherf. "This camp also has a public school. The road to that school cannot be closed to the public. Would you like me to cite that law as well, Captain?"

Scherf's fingers drum the hard leather of his holster, and he strains as he says "No, I would not!"

Beranek cries out from the crowd, "Some of our children go to that school, I'll have you know. You have no right-"

Scherf draws his billy club out of its sheath, holding it erect. "I'm getting real sick of you rotten krauts, frogs, spics, and bohunks talking about your rights! You should be on your knees, thanking Lord Jesus, for us letting you come here and work! Taking our jobs! Robbing us blind!"

Davis steps out of the crowd, his shaking hands tight around his American flag. "Oh yeah?" he says, "I think us krauts and bohunks could teach you a thing or two about rights. Freedom of speech. Freedom to assemble. If you ask me, the real Americans are on *this* side of the gate!"

The leather on Scherf's billy club twists in his grip, and his eyes contort in their sockets, from wide as pocket-watches, to narrow as knife-slits.

"Come a little closer, boy, I didn't catch that."

As Scherf stares down Davis, Bell comes forward all the way, and rests his hand on the fence. "With all due respect, Captain, enough with the stunts. Let us in."

Scherf seizes Bell's hand, yanking him off-balance, and swings hard. The blow connects to Bell's face with a crack, knocking him backwards into the dirt.

A crowd of five hundred lurches forward in unison, and in an instant every Ranger's holster is unstrapped. A Ranger uselessly pumps his shotgun, ejecting an unspent slug to the ground. Spanudakhis and Davis lift Bell to his feet, clutching the left side of his face, looking back at Scherf with one eye.

Scherf steps back from the fence and yells, "Anyone comes over that gate, we'll carry you out!"

"Gimme that flag!" shouts a Ranger, and he grabs at Davis' flag through the fence. A tug-o-war ensues, drawing a crowd on either side. As the crowd of picketers surges toward the fence, Bell finds himself being pushed face-first into the barbed wire, stumbling boots crushing his broken glasses. In self-preservation, he begins climbing the fence, pulling others up alongside him. As Bell comes over the top, he pricks his thumb on a barb, and is stopping to suck on it when he is pulled over to the Ranger's side. The clubs are coming down on his back before he even hits the ground.

There is a mighty heave from the picketers, pulling Davis' flag back to their side. Beranek grabs a flag from Spanudakhis' hands, and, undeterred by her long dress, scales the fence, landing on the other side. She covers Bell's unconscious body with the flag, surely pride in that flag is something everyone here still shares.

"Gentlemen, please," she says, "come to your senses!"

A club strikes Beranek in the face, a circle of Rangers landing heavy kicks and blows on her and Bell. In the maelstrom, the flag comes off of Bell, trampled in the icy mud.

The sad sight of Mrs. Beranek is too much for the picketers. Another surge pushes the miners against the gate, barbed wire be damned, and soon the half-ton structure is swaying back and forth, creaking and groaning in its muddy foundations.

Scherf and the Rangers look up from Bell and Beranek's bodies, watching the gate teeter and moan.

"Orders, Captain!" shouts a Ranger.

"Fall back, men!" says Scherf. His eyes scan the surging crowd. "Do you see any of them carrying weapons? Come on, give me something to work with!"

"Nothing, sir!"

Scherf storms forward, kicking Bell again. "Dammit! Gas 'em, now! Drive 'em back!"

The Rangers pull gas canisters from their belts, tug the pins out, and toss them over the fence. A sickly, yellow gas fans out amongst the miners. Jacques feels his throat close up, eyes blinded by flowing water.

"Tear gas!" gasps Jacques, "throw it back!" Spanudakhis takes the last available gulp of fresh air, dives into the gas, and snatches the spewing canister, hurling it back over to the Rangers. Scherf is watching his second tossed canister fall into the thick of the crowd as his first can lands back at his feet. He shields his face, to no effect, and stumbles away hacking and retching.

Bell rises back into consciousness, and opens his eyes, sore joints nipping at him for every move he tries to make. He looks up in terror, grabs Beranek, and pulls her out of the way just as the swaying front gate of the Columbine topples over, collapsing in a twisted heap with a rending crash of metal.

Scherf falls to the ground, wiping his eyes with his shirt sleeve. He sees silhouettes form in the yellow clouds, materializing into the strikers, the chants of Solidarity throbbing through them and driving them onward. He gets back to his feet, taking another step back, and jumps as he feels the wall of the Foreman's office behind him. Scherf curses aloud, pounding the office siding with his fist.

"We've gone back far enough!" screams Scherf. He fumbles for his holster, drawing his Colt 1911, eyes red and mouth drooling from the tear gas. He aims his gun skyward.

"Don't come any closer!" he cries, and he fires two rounds into the air.

The crack of the gun makes the other Rangers whip their heads around. Scherf hears the sound of sliding bolts, cocking hammers, and cylinders primed.

"You heard the Captain!" shouts a Ranger. "Ready! Aim!"

Scherf spins around to the Ranger, "No, wait-!"

In the cold dawn, the valleys of the coal field echo with roaring thunder. There is a great silence, and the whistle at the Columbine blows three times.

CHAPTER TWELVE

No Place That Far

"Bang! Bang! I got you, Wobbly!"

Ortega watches the two boys run around him in the Union Hall, their tiny fingers held like guns.

"Take that, company man!" says the other boy, "Bang-bang!"

They fling the front door open and run out into the street. Beranek watches them on the front step, her hand still frozen in a knocking pose. She was hoping she wouldn't find Ortega here again, ledger in hand, as he has been for the past three days. Thanksgiving has come at last.

Beranek's face is bruised and bandaged, her eyes distant. Like Ortega, the shock and agony of that morning three days ago has been cast into her like concrete. Even here on Simpson Street, with Thanksgiving feast imminent, she still feels like she's back inside the Columbine's gate, ears ringing from the gunfire, looking up to see Davis sprawled out on the road in a pool of blood. Life had entered suspension, and every moment was a reliving of that horror.

Ortega drops his pencil onto the ledger. "Mrs. Beranek" says Ortega.

"How are you doing?" she asks.

"Mary and *mis hijos* are okay. Mrs. Lewis at the boarding house is looking after them now. They'll be safe there. And no whooping cough."

Beranek feigns a smile, but it's soon gone. "The coroner has his report," she says.

"I saw" says Ortega.

Eastenes is dead, so are Spanudakhis and Jacques. Davis died on the way to the hospital, along with two more men. Dozens had been injured, men and women alike, but no children. In the chaos, Beranek didn't know what had happened to Bell, and the Sheriff's deputies had described his condition as "missing."

"So Mike didn't make it," says Ortega. "Jacques used to talk about him. Six dead. Just makes things more complicated."

"Beg pardon?" says Beranek.

Ortega looks down at his ledger. "I just can't organize it all neat. We needed an Orthodox funeral for Nick, a Catholic funeral for Jacques in Louisville, and now this Mike fellow in Erie, - *ay, muy complicado*, we'll need a military funeral for him. Did you know he fought in the Great War? I don't know any bugle players, do you?" Beranek shakes her head. "We need them to do that thing, that thing, you know, where they play the bugle at the funeral, ah, *como se dice*, that song they play…"

"I know," says Beranek. Everyone in town was like this now, trying to drown themselves in busy work, rambling on as long as possible to avoid being alone with their pain.

"I know, of course you know," says Ortega.

Beranek comes up to Ortega and closes the ledger for him. "I can come by later to help plan. Good Lord, Bertha has six kids, they'll need help with food. I think Mrs. Lewis said her husband still has some credits over at the Hayward Mine, maybe I can send him over for supplies." Beranek heads for the door.

"You're better at this than me, Mrs. Beranek," Ortega calls out after her. He strikes a boxing pose, fists raised. "Maybe I can sell autographed photos, *si*?

Beranek smiles at him, and closes the Union Hall door behind her. Out on the doorstep, she takes out a handkerchief, drying her eyes. She stays there a good long time before making her way to the boarding house.

Ortega stands in the Union Hall, alone. "Yes," he says to himself, "take your picture with Johnny Kid Mex. Defending featherweight champion of the Rockies. Defending champion. Defending..."

He stops, looking down at a box on the desk. He sets the ledger aside, and reaches into the box, pulling out a length of crumpled cloth. Ortega unfolds the cloth, staring at Davis' American flag. Unpresentable now, all shot full of holes, the young man's bloodstains turning a dark mahogany. He lowers the flag back into the box, and sets the box off on another table. Silence in the hall.

The boxer cries out, lifting his fists over his head, and with ferocious speed, slams them onto the desk. The desk shakes and bends under the force, and Ortega brings his full rage to bear, throwing a torrent of punches and kicks against the wood. Years in the fighting ring, of being pushed into peak condition in the crucible of the mines, are distilled into this moment of sheer fury, as the desk is ripped apart by his blows.

A final kick, and Ortega collapses against the shattered remains of the desk, sobbing. He searches his memories, and can't remember ever seeing his own father cry. Perhaps his father also waited until he was alone.

* * * *

A day's journey to the south, Flaming Mamie sits in her jail cell, her red dress unfaded even with her second arrest. A guard comes up, dangling a set of keys.

"This being a holiday, and all," says the guard, "Any chance we can release you early, so we can get home for dinner? The judge says all he needs from you is an apology."

Flaming Mamie turns away from the guard, lying back on her wooden bench. "I have nothing to apologize for," she says. "There's still work to be done."

* * * *

Back up north, in Weld County, the cell door slides open, and Bell watches a train ticket fall into his lap. Sheriff Robinson stands at the open door.

"It's on me, Adam. Tell anyone and I'll deny it."

Bell takes the ticket, his stiff body rising up off the cot. His bruised ribs still leave him short of breath, but he makes his way out of the cell, the Sheriff following.

"You're a drifter and a troublemaker," says the Sheriff. "Maybe someday, Adam, you can drift yourself somewhere far from police or picket lines."

Bell laughs, and the bruised ribs punish him for it. "A place without police or pickets?" he asks. "A place without cold tenement rows, or Rangers? There's no place that far away.

I think I'll find my way to those places as long as there's breath in my body."

* * * *

At the State Capitol in Denver, Governor Adams is delivering a radio address from his office. The press copy down his words, and Jesse Welborn looks on from a corner of the room.

The Governor recites, "My reports show conclusively that the strikers were to blame for Monday's affair. Captain Scherf exercised great patience, and wonderful courage, doing everything possible to avoid bloodshed."

Welborn checks his watch, straightens his suit, and heads for the door. He can't keep his family waiting for Thanksgiving dinner. Long ago, he had asked John Rockefeller if those pressures that turn iron into steel had the same effect on men. Now he believes he knows the answer.

With the address finished, the press and radio technicians leave the office, and the Governor's secretary closes the door behind her. Adams leans back in his chair, pulls his cowboy hat off the coat rack, and drops it over his face. A month later, he will announce his retirement from public office.

* * * *

Elsewhere in Denver, Louis Scherf stands outside of a club, listening to the wild commotion inside. He pulls a flask out of his jacket, and takes a long drink. He takes a deep breath before opening the door, and soon the crowd inside is clamoring for Captain Scherf, the hero of the hour, hip-hip, hooray! The other Rangers invite him inside to sample a new beer keg, confiscated from Central City.

* * * *

On the floor of Lafayette's Union Hall, Ortega mops the tears from his eyes with a rag, licking his bloodied knuckles. Five minutes pass, and Ortega tosses the broken desk into the back alley, ready to prepare the hall for Thanksgiving feast.

CHAPTER THIRTEEN

Thanksgiving

The frenzied dancing that once filled Union Hall is far away as the town of Lafayette gathers in the same room for Thanksgiving. The hall is hushed as plates of turkey, cranberry, and yam are passed around. Across the long banquet table, six chairs stand empty. An empty chair sits to the left of old Mrs. Jacques. It seemed like all of Louisville came out to her boy's funeral, the papers counted it at 1,500 people.

At Jacques' funeral, the priest had quoted John, Chapter 14, *"Let not your heart be troubled... if I go and prepare a place for you, I will come again, and receive you unto myself; that where I am, there ye may be also."* Mrs. Jacques imagines her firstborn son, Frank, preparing a place for her little Rene: the pitiless abyss where Frank had been bludgeoned by the mule's hooves. Now they had both been cast into the frigid November earth.

Another empty chair sits next to Bertha and her children. Dorothy wears the dress Eastenes had bought her. The room is quiet for a long time, save for the passing of plates and clatter of silverware. Beranek looks up from her plate at Dorothy, who pokes at a wad of cranberry with her fork.

"That's a lovely dress, Dorothy."

Bertha puts an arm around her daughter. "Thank you," says Dorothy. "I was saving it for when I would sing at Christmas mass."

"Your Daddy always loved your singing," says Bertha.

Ortega sits a few chairs away, holding Mary and his children in his arms. His lips mouth at voiceless words, none of which seem to fit, until he peeks down the line of guests to Dorothy.

"Dorothy, I don't know if your *padre* ever told you about the time he taught me how to sing."

"He did?" asks Dorothy.

"*Si*, he said it was a song he'd taught you. *Lead, Kindly Light. Usted sabe?*"

Dorothy thinks for a second, and closes her eyes. Her soft voice fills the hall, and as she sings in the low candlelight, Ortega remembers that long walk home.

"Lead, kindly light, amidst the encircling gloom,

The night is dark, I'm far from home,

Keep thou my feet, I do not ask to see

The distant scene, one step enough for me."

Dorothy draws her breath, and with the next verse, finds Ortega singing with her, then Mary, then Beranek, and Bertha, and Mrs. Jacques, and her mom and brothers and sisters, one by one.

"So long thy power hath blest me, lead me on,

O'er moor and fen, 'til night is gone,

And with the morn, those angel faces smile

Which I have loved long since and lost a while..."

The men and women in the Union Hall look around to find themselves surrounded by each other's voices, the song envelops them, and fills the empty spaces of the hall. They recognize the feeling as the same one they felt when they danced here, a week ago, united by Flaming Mamie's call for freedom. It was the feeling from that night when, under the first snowfall, they listened to the song about the boy on the lake shore, and their decision to act in the face of a hopeless future. It was the same feeling the miners knew deep in those tunnels, where old mules, falling rock, and raging fire were faced together, with faith in your fellow man.

The night is dark, I'm far from home, or so the hymn went. *One step enough for me.*

The Union Hall is still reverberating with the old hymns as the families begin clearing plates away. From the back of the hall, three visitors, a vampire and two boys, step out of the shadows, invisible to the families as they go about their work.

Gerry looks around the scene, and whispers, "Wow... this all really happened. Right in our back yard..."

Sean watches the Ortegas, Beraneks, and Eastenes carry food back to the kitchen. "I guess this isn't such a boring place after all, but all that pain and suffering, it's horrible."

Glava nods. "Yes, this story is a painful one, but look at these people. I see a city united as one. This tragedy has bound them together in ways we can never imagine."

"What happened to the miners?" asks Gerry.

"One year later," says Glava, "the Columbine Mine became the first in Colorado to sign a union agreement. The new owner, Josephine Roche, even chose a survivor of Ludlow, named John Lawson, as her vice-president. She then went to Washington to work for President Roosevelt, and in 1933, the right to unionize became national law. After all the years of strikes and bloodshed, the voice of the Colorado coal miner had been heard at last.

"They had so little, but were thankful for so much. In the deepest mine shafts, the coldest winters, or the hungriest strikes, they found comfort in friends and loved ones. Their lives were filled with music and dance, with laughter and love. Like the first Pilgrims to America, they left behind a life in the old world for a chance to build a new one, if not for themselves, then for their children. They believed in something that didn't even have a name yet: the American Dream."

Glava takes a candle off the banquet table, looking into the flame. All around, the spirits of the cemetery begin blowing the candles out, the room darkening each time.

Glava looks up from the candle. "This story is finished. Whatever power it has is up to you. We are only spirits, our presence is as permanent as ripples on a lake, as enduring as footprints in a snowstorm. We can only ask you to remember. Remember, that in the rolling hills east of the Rockies, a group of brave men and women risked everything, to stand up for what was right."

The vampire cups his hands around the candle and puffs it out. There is darkness in the hall, but a new light has been lit, leading them on, one step at a time.

EPILOGUE

or, What's Past Is Prologue

Sean and Gerry open their eyes, and back out of the way of a beige sedan, headed home from the Bob Burger Recreation Center. On the front walkway, the giant inflatable turkey sways in the November wind before a graying sky. Across the parking lot, middle-schoolers navigate their way through the bowls and rails of the skate park. The baseball diamond lies empty, and toddlers run giddy toward piles of cottonwood leaves.

The two watch the first wisps of snow begin to touch the grass of the cemetery, and dust the headstones with the finest film of white. The stories of the departed who lay here, stories of success, hardship, war, heartache, frustration, surprise, wonder, pain, courage, compassion, all joys and all sorrows, gone, save for two numbers: the year of their birth, and the year of their death.

All at once, the unfathomable depths of the past seem to Sean and Gerry like a vast and terrible ocean, ready to drown their pitiful existences under the weight of all those who had come before. With that terror, though, came the hope that this vast ocean could be sailed, with charts to guide them, and currents to carry them toward isles of discovery they could not even begin to glimpse.

At the northeast end of the skate park, the trees spread apart, and in the far distance, through the falling snow, are those low, rolling hills where the Columbine once stood. The hills loom over the valley, once called the coal field, covered in that same dry grass the miners trudged through all those years ago.

Sean rubs his palms together and blows into his cupped hands. Neither of them is dressed for this kind of weather. They agree to meet up in Louisville tomorrow for hockey, say goodbye, and they both feel the same sensation that the story may not be quite over. In fact, it may have just begun.

The snow is falling harder as the boys hurry home.

THE END

CREDITS

America the Beautiful lyrics by Katherine Lee Bates, from her poem *America, A Poem for July 4*, 1904.

Where the Columbines Grow lyrics by A.J. Flynn, 1915.

Lead, Kindly Light lyrics by John Henry Newman, from his poem *Pillar of Cloud*, 1833.

ABOUT THE AUTHOR

Nicholas Bernhard is a writer, composer, and documentary filmmaker. He directed the acclaimed documentary *Blackstone's Equation: The Tim Masters Story*, about Colorado's most notorious wrongful conviction case. Since 2017, he has written the monthly column *Tales of the Northern Coal Field* for Yellow Scene Magazine.

Mr. Bernhard lives in Colorado.

Nicholas@NDHFilms.com

ABOUT THE ILLUSTRATOR

The maps in this edition were illustrated by cartoonist Mister V. His comics *Life is Grand* and *Them There Hills* cover the history and wildlife of Colorado, and are published in the Grand Gazette newspaper.

Arborcides.com

Fields

Northern Coal Field
200 Miles North

PUEBLO

Arkansas River

The Great Plains

AGUILAR

Ludlow Tent Colony
"The White City"

TRINIDAD